STALKER *girl*

STALKER girl

ROSEMARY GRAHAM

SCHOLASTIC INC.
New York Toronto London Auckland
Sydney Mexico City New Delhi Hong Kong

ISBN 978-0-545-39025-5

12 11 10 9 8 7 6 5 4 3 2 1   11 12 13 14 15 16/0

Printed in the U.S.A.   .   40

First Scholastic printing, September 2011

Book design by Nancy Brennan
Set in Berling

To my daughter,
Graham Griffin

PART
one

SHE WAS even prettier in person.

She wore her straight brown hair clipped up in a loose twist. A few stray strands fell against her long, elegant neck. Her clingy yoga clothes—a blue, low-cut, long-sleeved T-shirt over cropped black pants—showed off a tight and curvy body. When she crossed the café, people couldn't help but check her out.

Some more obviously than others:

That hipster guy at the back table sitting in front of his laptop, rubbing his thumb back and forth over his stubbly soul patch; the skinny hipster girl with the peroxide pig-tails sitting next to the guy with the soul patch, scowling; the teenage boy busing tables; that father with the cute toddler twins and the very tired-looking wife.

And sitting on a stool by the window, an open note-book by her side, wearing an ugly brown knit hat and a bizarre pair of turquoise glasses, another girl, somewhere around the same age as the pretty brown-haired one.

If you knew Carly Finnegan and you happened to see her sitting on that stool by the window, watching the girl, you wouldn't suspect her of any wrongdoing. Certainly not anything criminal. If you knew Carly well enough to know that she no longer lived just ten but more like a hundred blocks away, you might wonder for a second what she was doing all the way downtown. But then if you knew her well enough to know where she lived and where she used to live, you'd also know that she had a seven-year-old half sister whose father still lived on Fourteenth Street. If you knew all this, you'd probably know or guess that the task of escorting Jess downtown to see her father sometimes fell on Carly's shoulders.

Which made it perfectly possible that she'd happen to stop in at the café where Taylor Deen, her ex-boyfriend's new girlfriend, was having coffee with her mother after the Saturday Salutations class at Studio Shakti across the street.

There was only one person in the city of New York who would find it odd for Carly and Taylor to be in the same café at the same time, and he was never up this early on a Saturday morning. Carly knew—she had checked and double-checked online—that Brian's band still played their regular Friday-night gig at Train. Which meant his head wouldn't have hit his pillow in Brooklyn until four a.m., and no way would he be on this side of the East River this side of noon.

Even if it was true that he was "totally whacked" for this new girl.

As unlikely as it was that Brian would appear that morning, Carly had still taken precautions. She'd stuffed the long, unruly red hair Brian claimed to love so much under a scratchy wool hat she found at the bottom of a Goodwill-destined bag in her mother's closet and bought a cheap pair of funky turquoise reading glasses in the lowest available power. She felt pretty safe hiding in plain sight, sneaking surreptitious glances at his new girlfriend, scribbling in her notebook. Her stool by the window was carefully chosen for the view it offered of the entire café and its proximity to the door. If necessary, she could slip out and disappear in seconds.

All she had wanted was a glimpse, a clear look at the face that belonged to the name that was now paired with Brian's. The three measly pictures she'd found online were worthless—one too old, the next too blurry, and the third nothing more than a thumbnail showing one eye, half a nose, and all those perfect, white teeth.

Carly had gotten her glimpse earlier that morning. She'd staked out the Deen family's brownstone until Taylor and her mother, Judith, emerged. She'd watched as the two of them walked arm in arm up the street and around the corner. But when they disappeared into the yoga studio, Carly realized that one glimpse wasn't going to be enough. She checked the schedule posted out front and returned an hour later, when the Saturday Salutations class ended. (FOR LEVELS 3 & 4 ONLY; MUST HAVE PERMISSION FROM SHAKTI TO ATTEND!) Carly hovered across the street, pretending to talk on her cell phone while keeping an eye on the mother-daughter pair as they mingled with the other yoga elites. When they crossed the street and entered Café Joe, she followed.

Carly knew what people would say if they knew what she was doing.

"That's crazy."

"That's creepy."

"That's just sad."

While she was sure she wasn't the only dumped person ever to track down the new love interest of an ex, she knew she was flirting with danger. Her curiosity was turning into something else. Not to mention how much time she was wasting.

And so Carly promised herself that when Taylor and her mother left the café, she would, too. Whichever way they were walking, she'd walk in the other direction.

Without looking back.

After all, she had a life. She had friends.

She would put the past behind her and walk forward into the wide-open future.

But first, as long as she was there, she'd play Harriet the Spy a little while longer. Study this mother-daughter duo in their native habitat.

She put pen to paper and entered the following data:

Time of arrival: approx. 10:08.
Apparel:
T.D.—Black wide-legged yoga pants. Blue long-sleeved shirt. Long deep-red sweater.
J.D.—Tailored black coat (cashmere?), blue print scarf (silk?).

From her perch Carly watched as Taylor bantered with the baristas, two guys and a girl. She could tell from the way Taylor stood with her arms casually resting on the chrome countertop, laughing while they pulled espresso shots and steamed milk, that she was a regular.

When Taylor crossed the room to join her mother at their table, a tall frothy something in each hand, she seemed oblivious to the eyes that followed her.

But Carly wondered whether she was truly oblivious. Was this one of those cases where you're so used to being looked at, you pretend not to notice?

For a while, all Taylor did was text while her mother read the *New York Times*. Carly watched her sitting there, smiling at her BlackBerry, thumbs flying over its little keyboard. She wondered if Brian was the recipient and cringed when she remembered her last conversation with him, his threat to change his number.

Eventually Taylor put the BlackBerry aside. For most of the next hour, she sat there reading the paper and talking with her mother. Once in a while one of them would share something interesting, and they'd discuss. They worked on the crossword puzzle together until they gave up, laughing. People—other café regulars—stopped by their table, and there'd be more chatter, more laughter. At one point Taylor took a call on her BlackBerry, and instead of going outside for privacy, she kept interrupting the conversation to fill her mother in.

Apparently the sort of mother-daughter chumminess Carly thought existed only in small, made-for-TV towns lived in the heart of Greenwich Village.

From across the room Carly couldn't hear anything they were saying. But she could tell from their facial expressions and body language that this mother and daughter liked each other, enjoyed each other's company.

When a stool closer to their table opened up, she moved over. Now she could hear bits and pieces of the conversation. Carly kept up the pretense of intense angsty journaling while writing down what words she could make out.

She made two columns and put each one's words in the proper place.

Judith	*Taylor*
dinner	seventeen
muscles (or mussels?)	Tuesday
your father	chocolate
yes	I think so
last night	with Brian

Just when things were getting interesting, a guy sat down on the next stool and started making calls without the least effort to keep the volume down. First he called his mother to tell her he wouldn't be able to come by that morning as he had said he might. He was really sorry, but he was just too bogged down with work. Yeah. Uh-huh. The Something Something Case. Huge case. Huge. Boss needed him all day.

There was nothing remotely resembling work in front of this guy. Just a *Daily News* open to the sports page and a book called *Surfing Australia*. After he got off the phone with Mom, he called someone he greeted as "bruh" and made plans to shoot hoops in an hour.

When the lying, surfing, hoops-shooting bruh finally shut up and settled in to reading the sports section, Carly heard Judith say, "You won't forget about tonight."

She looked up to see Taylor standing, buttoning up her deep-red sweater. "Of course not. What time are they coming?"

"Seven thirty. Want me to call and remind you?"

She shrugged. "I'm not going to be able to do anything once the sunlight's gone." She walked around the table and stood behind her mother with a hand on each shoulder. "But if it makes you feel better, sure, call me." She leaned down. Judith smiled and closed her eyes as her daughter planted a kiss on her cheek.

Taylor stepped away and held out a hand. Her mother placed the long leather strap of a big, expensive, and complicated-looking camera on it. "Thanks," Taylor said, slipping the strap over her neck and shoulder so it lay diagonally across the red sweater, between her breasts.

Carly really didn't want to look at Taylor Deen's breasts, but she found it impossible not to look, impossible not to compare.

They weren't huge. Probably a B, same as her. But still they seemed fuller, rounder. Like everything else about this girl and this girl's life—better than Carly's.

As she stepped away from the table, her mother held out her coffee mug. "Honey, will you ask Bess to start another one for me on your way out?"

"Sure," Taylor said, taking the mug. "Don't forget my mat." She tilted her head toward the Shakti Yoga bag slung over the back of her chair and headed toward the counter to talk to Bess.

Wait! Carly wanted to say. *You haven't finished your croissant. Come on. Hang out a little while longer.*

Carly stuffed her notebook in her messenger bag, grabbed her hoodie, and dashed for the door, slipping out while Taylor ordered her mother's refill.

Oh, she hadn't forgotten her promise. She still had every intention of walking the other way. To do that, of course, she'd need to know which way Taylor was going. So she stopped on the sidewalk and pretended to fiddle with the clasps on her bag while she waited. When Taylor still hadn't come out, Carly turned her back to the door and adjusted her ugly hat. Finally, from over her shoulder she heard the swish of the door opening. She took two long, slow breaths before turning back around to see Taylor heading down Fourth Street toward Washington Square. The red of her sweater stood out amidst the mostly-black-wearing denizens of Greenwich Village. She was moving fast, like she had somewhere to be. Like someone was expecting her.

Carly looked down at her feet. She was standing right between two sidewalk lines. If she turned to her left and walked up Fourth Street, she could get on the subway at Sixth Avenue and head uptown. She could spend her Saturday doing normal, healthy, constructive things, like finally tackling that essay she had to write for her one college application. Or she could work on her history paper about the Triangle Factory Fire. She was due at work at five, and work was always fun.

If she chose to turn right, she knew full well she'd be choosing trouble. She'd already spent enough time obsessing about Brian and then, after she heard there was someone new, tracking down every detail she could find about Taylor Deen and her semifamous Greenwich Village family.

It was time to stop. Carly knew that. *She had a life. She had friends.*

She raised her head, took a deep breath and a tentative half step left, toward the rest of her life. But then out of the corner of her eye she caught a glimpse of that red sweater, and she went the other way.

2

CARLY HADN'T set foot in Washington Square Park since the move. She'd walked by and around it a few times, after leaving Jess for her weekends at Nick's, but hadn't been able to walk through. Doing so would only increase her feeling of exile. Crossing the patch of trees and grass and asphalt she'd crossed thousands of times would dredge up the happy, irretrievable past. But when Taylor headed into the park, Carly followed.

Taylor walked right up to the fence surrounding the dog run and started snapping pictures. Carly hung back and sidestepped her way over to a bench. She sat down, dug out her notebook, and resumed scribbling. She did her best to look like a homesick NYU student writing poems about loneliness while she watched Taylor snapping away at the happy-to-be-off-leash dogs chasing and charging each other around the fenced-in patch of open space.

Carly recognized one of them, an Australian shepherd named Oz, whose eyes were two different colors. She scanned the benches for Professor and Mrs. Jackson, Oz's

owners. Carly had gotten to know the older English couple years before, when she was so deep into her dog-loving
phase that she preferred the dog run to the playground.
She'd stay there as long as Nick or her mother would allow,
asking owners their dogs' names, ages, and breeds, petting
the ones who'd stand still long enough. Most owners toler-
ated Carly's insistent questions, some more grumpily than
others. But the Jacksons always seemed happy to see her
and eager to share stories about Oz. They always dressed
impeccably—Mrs. Jackson in a skirt, stockings, and sensi-
ble low-heeled shoes; Professor Jackson in a jacket (tweed
or seersucker, depending on the season) and bow tie. They
always sat on the same bench, drinking the milky tea they
always brought in an old thermos with a tartan plaid
exterior.

But only Professor Jackson was on the bench today. He
was wearing fall tweed and holding—Carly had to squint
to be sure—a blue-and-white take-out cup. Had something happened to Mrs. Jackson since Carly moved away?

Oz gamboled over to where Taylor stood and sniffed
at her knees.

Taylor waved to Professor Jackson, who lifted his cup
in greeting. Could Taylor know Professor Jackson? Had
Carly and Taylor already crossed paths at the dog run or
somewhere else in between the ten blocks that once sepa-
rated them? Could they have played together in the tot lot
when they were little?

That would be funny.

Or sad, depending on how you looked at things.

While Taylor talked to Professor Jackson, Carly's eyes wandered across the path to the playground, where a man was pushing a baby girl on the swing with one hand while reading the folded-up newspaper he held in the other. Carly thought he was pushing a little too hard for that small a baby. It made her nervous to see how the baby bounced when she reached the apex of the upswing. The father wasn't even watching. He too busy reading football scores or stock prices. The baby liked it just fine, though. She kicked her feet and waved her arms. Carly could hear her delighted squeals all the way over at her out-of-the-way bench.

When one of the baby's little red shoes fell to the ground, the father didn't notice. As Carly sat there debating whether she should run over and point out the missing shoe to the negligent father, Taylor swept in, scooped up the shoe from under the swinging baby, and offered it to him. He shoved the newspaper under his arm, stopped the swing, and put the shoe back on the baby's foot while Taylor took pictures. With the hot girl watching and recording his actions for posterity, the guy suddenly couldn't get enough of his progeny. He squeezed her thighs, pretended to chomp at her foot. Everything but the *goochy-goo*.

When Taylor waved good-bye, this Father of the Year candidate went right back to his old ways.

Taylor resumed a brisk pace as she headed for the fountain, where three firemen sat on the low concrete wall soaking up the sun, drinking Starbucks and laughing. One of them took his FDNY jacket off just as Taylor approached, conveniently revealing his broad shoulders and seriously hard arms.

When she aimed her camera at them, he elbowed the other guys and they started messing around, throwing their arms around each other's shoulders, raising their coffee cups like they were toasting someone's big news.

"No, no, don't pose." Taylor laughed. "Pretend I'm not here."

That cracked them up. "Oh yeah, right. We'll just pretend you're not here," said the buff one.

They kept right on mugging for the girl and her camera. She laughed along with them, took a few more shots, and then showed them the pictures on her camera. As she walked away, the weightlifter said, "Wait. I want a copy of that one. Lemme have your number."

"Okay," she said. "Two-one-two . . ."

This took him by surprise. "Whoa. Wait." He dug in his front pocket, pulled out his phone, and flipped it open. "Okay. Two-one-two . . ."

With a big smile, she said, "Five-five-five—"

The other two got it first. They smirked at each other and watched their friend enter, "Five-five—"

When it dawned on him that she was giving him an

obviously fake number, he shrugged, flipped his phone closed, and laughed along with his buddies.

Taylor laughed, too. Then she waved, turned around, and resumed her brisk pace. Carly followed.

When Carly passed the firemen, she heard Mr. Muscles say, "What? It was worth a shot." Then his eyes lit on Carly. "Hey," he said. "What's the rush? There a fire somewhere?"

She felt herself blush and walked faster, wishing she had Taylor's quick comeback skills or a sassy friend like Taylor by her side.

Carly followed Taylor all the way to Chinatown, ducking into doorways, pretending to window-shop or faking cell-phone conversations whenever Taylor stopped to take pictures. There were some close calls. She had to jaywalk a few times or risk losing sight of Taylor, and one particularly aggressive cabbie almost ran her down. And once, she was so focused on Taylor's red sweater that she didn't see a woman and her two small children until she bumped smack into them, almost knocking the woman to the ground.

She apologized. Profusely. "I'm sorry. I'm sorry. I'm so sorry," she said. But how sorry could Carly be if she didn't even come to a complete stop? She slowed down, and faced the woman, humbly accepting the woman's irate "What is wrong with you?" and "Why don't you watch where you're going?" as she walked backward. But she never stopped moving. After one more "I know" and "I'm so sorry," she turned her back on the woman and ran to make up the extra distance the incident had created between her and Taylor. She resolutely ignored the dirty looks she got from people who had witnessed the mishap.

Carly couldn't remember the last time she'd been in Chinatown. It was just past noon and the place was packed, the sidewalks brimming with people and stuff for sale.

One place sold only slippers. Black canvas slippers, red imitation-silk slippers embroidered in gold, assorted flip-flops bearing unfamiliar cartoon characters.

Then there was a row of fish shops. Everywhere she looked she saw whole, dead fish on ice. One store had a grimy box of half-dead frogs. At first Carly thought they were all-the-way dead, but then she saw their throats expanding like tiny balloons and their beady black eyes blinking in slow motion.

Taylor seemed to know a lot of the vendors. They greeted her with big smiles and nods as she went from store to store, taking pictures of them and their wares. In one shop, she knelt in front of a barrel of oranges; in the next she squatted by a giant ceramic cat; in another she shot an enormous bin full of CDs, all with the face of a beautiful Chinese woman peeking out from behind a bouquet of red roses. Next to the bin was a life-sized cardboard cut-out of the smiling woman, which Taylor also photographed.

As crowded as it was in Chinatown, Carly found it harder to hide. Most of the other non-Chinese people were tourists, busy buying imitation-silk slippers, mini Statues of Liberty, and various items declaring how much they ♥ed NY.

The vendors who greeted Taylor with such friendly smiles had only suspicious looks for Carly. When Taylor stopped in front of a steamy restaurant window and started taking pictures of the headless ducks under orange lights, Carly browsed the offerings of a produce stand next door, where an old woman sitting on a high stool by the cash register watched her every move. When the old woman said something to the young girl stocking shelves with cellophane-wrapped nests of dried noodles, the girl left her task to follow Carly.

Carly thought maybe if she bought something, they'd leave her alone. It would also give her something to do while she waited for Taylor to finish. She reached for a brown paper bag and filled it with a dark leafy thing she thought was bok choy. She wasn't sure because she'd only seen it cooked—and the sign, in Chinese characters, was no help. Whatever it was cost $1.99 a pound.

As she lifted each stalk into her bag, she'd sneak a peek over at Taylor, who was still with the ducks.

If she and Taylor were friends and on this expedition

together, this would be when she would say, *Hey! How many shots of dead ducks can you possibly need?* And Taylor would say something funny back, and together they would laugh at Mean Vegetable Lady.

When the bag was half full, Carly brought it to the old woman, who grunted, looked inside, and practically threw it on the scale. They both watched as the needle registered a measly three quarters of a pound.

Over the old woman's shoulder, Carly saw Taylor step away from the ducks and point her lens toward a long piece of some other kind of meat glistening in the restaurant window. The old woman turned to see what Carly was looking at and then turned back and said, "You're right. She has much better boobs. And she's prettier."

"Excuse me?"

"One dollar fifty-two cent," the woman repeated, annoyed.

"Oh," Carly said, as she handed the woman a ten. The woman reached into her apron pocket, took out a wad of bills, and counted out eight crumpled singles. She reached into the other pocket, fished out two quarters and practically slapped them into Carly's outstretched hand.

"Thank you," Carly whispered, and slunk away.

But now the only people in front of the restaurant window were four white-haired women in pantsuits trying to decide whether to venture into Lucky Flower Food. Two were reading the menu posted by the door; another peered nervously through the glass. One brave soul marched up to the door and pulled it open, beckoning the others to join her.

Carly tried not to panic as she looked around for the red sweater. A bus parked along the sidewalk was releasing more white-haired ladies into the wilds of Chinatown.

Finally, just as she was about to give up, Carly spotted Taylor standing in front of a jewelry store next to the restaurant, talking to a Chinese man in a business suit. Something about the way he was standing—with his feet apart, hands behind his back—and sizing up everyone who walked by made Carly think he was the owner. Taylor was talking fast, moving her hands a lot, like she was telling a complicated story. The man was nodding and smiling. Was it possible that Taylor was speaking Chinese? Was that another of her many talents?

Carly glanced back over her shoulder to see Mean Vegetable Lady glaring. She looked right into Carly's eyes and shook her head.

Carly's father once had a wacky New Age girlfriend who believed the universe sent her very specific, personal messages on a regular basis. When she had two car accidents in one week, the universe was telling her to take a vacation. In Europe. (Not, apparently, to take a refresher driver's ed class.) When her roof leaked into her clothes closet, it was the universe's way of telling her she needed to change her look. Toss everything out and start over. It was while she was in the middle of that makeover that she decided to break up with Carly's father, who seemed more relieved than anything. He'd dated some strange ones, but Cosmic Katie was the strangest.

Now Carly was thinking maybe Katie was on to something. Because she had the distinct impression that Mean Vegetable Lady was her own personal messenger from the universe, telling her to *stop*, *just stop* whatever it was she thought she was doing.

IT'S CRAZY!

IT'S CREEPY!!

IT'S JUST SAD!!!!!! ☹ ☹ ☹ ☹

The universe was right. Or mostly right. Following your ex-boyfriend's new girlfriend was creepy. And sad. She wasn't ready to concede crazy, but she could see how others might see it that way. Val, for example. If Val knew where she was right then, and why she was there, she'd probably come downtown herself and drag Carly away.

Carly knew she should stop. It was a beautiful, unusually warm Saturday morning in late November. And there were so many normal things a normal girl her age could be doing: sleeping, browsing college Web sites, homework. Even harmlessly cyber-stalking a new crush or an ex or an ex's new crush in the safety of her own bedroom would be normal.

But there she was, actually for-real stalking her ex-boyfriend's new girlfriend. She'd started out wanting just one glimpse of the girl, and next thing she was following her around the streets of Manhattan, ducking into doorways to avoid detection, buying unidentified vegetables for cover, and almost knocking over small children in her determination to stay on Taylor's trail.

Carly knew all this, and yet she didn't stop. She couldn't stop. She could see how Brian would be totally whacked for this girl. She was herself a little bit totally whacked for this girl. She could imagine spending the day by Taylor's side rather than behind her. She wanted to compare impressions of the pervy dad back on the playground and make fun of the muscle-bound fireman. She wanted to know how you got to be friends with Chinatown merchants. She wanted to go to yoga with Taylor and her mother and have coffee with them afterward. Carly was good at crosswords. They might have finished if she'd been helping them.

Carly didn't heed the universe's warning.

But she didn't ignore the warning altogether. Mean Vegetable Lady's scowling glare reminded her of the danger involved, the disaster it would be if she was discovered. So she decided to buy herself a new disguise. She looked at one merchant's array of hats and picked the one she hated the most—a pink-and-white-checked I ♥ NY trucker cap. A few stalls over, someone was selling knockoff designer

sunglasses. Carly chose a huge pair of fake Dolce & Gab-
banas with a gold-covered plastic DG on each side. She
stuffed the brown hat and turquoise glasses into her bag
and checked her image in the small hand mirror that the
merchant, eager to make a sale, held up for her.

"Very nice. Very pretty," he said, nodding and smiling.
"You look like Paris Hilton."

She didn't look anything like Paris Hilton.

But she didn't look anything like herself, either.

"I'll take them," she said.

3

FROM CHINATOWN Carly followed Taylor through the neighborhoods of the Lower East Side. She stayed across the street and half a block behind as they passed through the old Jewish shopping district, where Taylor stopped once to take pictures of a lingerie store window filled with what looked like hundreds of bras displayed on hundreds of headless torsos.

Taylor stopped again a few blocks later when she came upon a group of Dominican girls hanging out in front of a restaurant, El Castillo de Tito. Judging by the orthodontia and varying states of development, Carly figured they were twelve, maybe thirteen. At first, like the firemen in Washington Square Park, they hammed it up for the camera. They jutted their hips and shoulders, puckered their lips. But when Taylor spoke to them in fluent Spanish, they relaxed back into what they were doing before she arrived. Some danced to the reggaeton blaring from Tito's open door. Two sat on steps with a magazine between them, flipping pages, pointing and laughing. One girl braided another's hair while talking to a boy leaning out of a window a few floors above.

All the while, Taylor clicked away, moving from girl to girl, from English to Spanish and back.

When she finished, the girls gathered around while she showed them the pictures on her camera. They oohed and aahed, laughed and teased each other. Before leaving, Taylor got out her BlackBerry and took down the information they shouted at her, promising to let them know when she posted the pictures.

On a gentrified block of designer boutiques and expensive upscale restaurants, Taylor entered a tiny, below-ground restaurant. Carly crossed the street and, pulling her I ♥ NY cap down on her forehead, walked by to see Taylor sitting at the counter, studying a menu. She'd taken off her sweater, and her camera sat on the empty stool next to her.

By now it was almost two. Carly hadn't eaten anything since the bagel she and Jess split on their way downtown early that morning. She decided to wait for Taylor in the old-style coffee shop next door, where she hoped to find something cheap to eat.

Carly stood by the PLEASE WAIT TO BE SEATED sign while a fifty-something bleached-blonde waitress sat on a stool near the cash register. A smiling Oprah beamed out from the cover of the magazine she held in her lap, promising "A Joy-Filled Celebration of the Season."

"Excuse me, is it okay if I sit at that table by the window?"

Without looking up, the waitress said, "Suit yourself. Grill's closed till four."

"That's okay," Carly said sheepishly.

When the waitress finally sighed her way over to her table, Carly ordered the cream of broccoli soup.

The waitress rolled her eyes as she scribbled on her pad. "That it?"

"Some water?" Despite Carly's best efforts to sound grateful, she'd obviously ruined the waitress's day, if not her life.

Carly dug in her messenger bag for her Harriet the Spy notebook, placing the crumpled bag of bok choy on the table. She would spend the time filling in the route Taylor had taken around the city.

T.D. Departs Café Joe @ 11:08, walks east on 4th.
Enters WSP approx. 11:15, exits 11:45 via Washing. Pl. to B'way.
Walks south arrives Canal St. approx. 12:30.
E. on Canal to Orchard, N. on Orchard to Rivington.

But when she looked up, she saw Taylor sauntering up the steps of the place next door. She quickly closed the notebook, stuffed it and her new hat and sunglasses into her bag, and began to slide out of the booth just as the waitress arrived with the soup.

"Last door on your right."

Carly looked at her blankly.

"Bathroom's last door on your right."

"Oh. I'm sorry," she said. "I have to go. It's, um, an emergency."

"Okay," said the waitress as she reached into her apron pocket. "Here's your check." She slapped it down on the table.

Carly shifted her eyes to the window. Taylor was no longer visible. If she didn't leave that instant, she'd run the risk of losing her trail. She had no choice but to bolt.

The first "Hey!" came as she reached the door. She didn't stop.

The second *"Hey!"*—louder and angrier—came as she stepped onto the sidewalk. She didn't stop. She couldn't stop. She had to keep her eye on Taylor, who was almost at the end of the block. If she stopped, if she so much as looked back, she might miss seeing which way Taylor went next.

"HEY, YOU FORGOT SOMETHING!"

Carly stopped and, without turning around, took a quick inventory. She had her messenger bag. Her notebook was in the messenger bag. Her phone was in her pocket. Her jacket? Did she leave her jacket? No. She was wearing her jacket.

Carly turned around just as something hit the side-walk. The brown bag. The waitress had thrown it hard enough that it skittered and bounced and tore open at Carly's feet. The bok choy, limp and wilted, flopped onto the sidewalk.

"Brat," the waitress said.

4

WHEN THE bok choy landed at her feet, Carly took off. She ran right into the middle of the street, directly in front of a cab that was going faster than it had seemed from the sidewalk. The cabbie slammed on his brakes, blared his horn, and yelled out his window, *"What are you trying to do, get yourself killed?"*

Even then Carly didn't stop. She just kept running. Across the street, around the corner, and five blocks to the Canal Street subway station, where she hopped onto an uptown train that brought her within a few blocks of Val's in Spanish Harlem.

She and Val always got ready for their Saturday-night shift at SJNY, the restaurant owned by Val's mother and uncle, together. Carly didn't have much in the girly-girl style she was supposed to wear to work, so she always just let Val pick something out from her vast array of swishy skirts, clingy tops, and dangly earrings. After Val got through with Carly's hair and makeup, Carly practically looked like one of the family. A pale and freckly, red-headed, blue-eyed member of the family.

Carly was glad Val was in the shower when she got there. That way she didn't have to look Val in the eye when she answered "Nothing" to Val's "What'd you do all day?"

Not exactly a lie, but it felt like one.

There'd been a time when Val and Carly had no secrets or lies between them.

Once, early in their friendship, Carly had tried lying to Val. It was a white lie. A totally harmless untruth told to spare Val's feelings. This was back in eighth grade, Val's first year at the Bellwin School when she and Carly were just getting to know each other, before Carly understood that Val wasn't the kind of person whose feelings needed sparing.

They were in algebra. Val was at the board demonstrating how she'd managed to solve the extra-credit problem no one else could figure out, and Celine Hardiman told Piper Peterson—loud enough for half the class to hear—that she'd seen Val's shoes in a Wal-Mart commercial.

"Or maybe it was Kmart. I don't know, one of the Marts." Piper had laughed as she always did when Celine tried to be funny, and they both sneered at Val when she walked back to her seat.

When Val asked Carly what that was all about, Carly

said something like they were making fun of how smart Val was. But Val took one look at Carly's face and knew that wasn't it. She pressed for the truth, and it only made her laugh.

After class Val went up to Celine and said, "Actually, they're from Payless. Buy two, get a third pair for half price. Bought them with my own money, too. And by 'my own money,' I mean money I earned doing this thing—you might have heard of it—it's called working."

Someday Carly would tell Val everything. Like she used to. And they'd laugh about it. Like they used to.

Hey, remember that time I went temporarily insane?

And you turned into Scary Stalker Girl? Oh, yeah. You were some kind of crazy. I'm so glad you're normal again! Ha! Ha!

Yeah, me too. Ha! Ha! Ha!

But Carly wasn't ready to get all confessional. Not again. Not yet.

As far as Val knew, Carly was avoiding all things having to do with Brian. Just one week before, she and Val had deleted all of his band's songs from Carly's iPod, every last one of his texts on her phone, and the pictures she had on her laptop. They'd made something of a ceremony of it after Carly finally admitted that he had broken up with her. For three weeks she'd managed to hide it from everyone—even her best friend (and in some ways even herself)—in the vain hope that it wasn't really a breakup, just a temporary break. But there came a point when Carly couldn't fool herself any longer. She told Val what had happened and asked for her help.

It felt good. And right. Carly promised Val she wouldn't contact Brian or go online looking for information about him or his band. "That boy is taking up too much rent-free space in your head," Val said. "It is eviction time."

But then, almost immediately after making her promise, Carly broke it.

Now she cleared a swath of the steamed-up mirror in Val's bathroom and pulled the Paris Hilton sunglasses out of her bag.

Val turned the water off, slid the shower curtain open, and laughed when she saw Carly in the sunglasses. "Where did you get *those*?"

"Chinatown," Carly said, putting her hand on her hip and thrusting a shoulder out. "I thought it was time for a new look. What do you think?"

"No offense, but they look terrible on you. They take up your whole face. Can you get me those towels?"

Carly grabbed two fluffy pink towels from the rack behind her and handed them to Val.

"When were you in Chinatown?"

"I . . . uh . . ." Carly turned her back and started undressing, trying to remember exactly what she'd already said about how she spent her day. "I just sort of wandered over there this afternoon." She hung her clothes on the doorknob and stepped into the shower at the back end of the tub as Val stepped out at the front.

Hidden safely behind the shower curtain, she said, "I had to take Jess down to Nick's, and I just felt like walking." She squeezed a glob of tropical-fruit-scented shampoo into her hair. If her voice betrayed anything, it was drowned out by the shower.

"Well, I'm confiscating them."

Carly peeked out from behind the curtain to find Val wrapped and crowned in pink towels and wearing the sunglasses. They looked good on her. The brown tint went with her skin tone and hair much better than with Carly's.

"Go ahead. Keep them."

"Thanks, dahling," Val said as she smacked air kisses on each side of Carly's wet face. "Come on, we'd better move it. We're going to get slammed tonight, thanks to J.Lo."

"J.Lo? Is she coming in tonight?"

"No, but she gave us a shout-out on the radio, and people have been calling all day for reservations."

Val's mother and uncle started SJNY—San Juan, New York—ten years earlier. For those ten years, it had been popular enough among the Spanish-speaking uptown population to make them a reasonable income and employ anyone in the family who needed a job. But a recent write-up in *New York* magazine had brought its popularity to a new level. Now the whole city knew about SJNY's "generous portions of tasty Puerto Rican fare"—the "zingy ceviche" and "tantalizingly seasoned stews and soups." People from all over the city lined up on Friday and Saturday nights to gorge on the cheap food and generous tropical drinks and to hear the live Latin jazz in the bar.

Val and Carly helped Val's mother, Angela, manage the door. They kept track of the waiting list and handed out menus. Sometimes, when things got really busy, they helped clear and set tables or deliver food.

The combination of Saturday plus a Jennifer Lopez endorsement plus the unseasonably warm weather meant, according to Val's cousin Luis, that they would be especially busy that night. He greeted the girls with an order for three hundred fruit garnishes—one slice each of pineapple and orange speared together with a paper umbrella—for all the fruity cocktails he'd be mixing later.

"Three hundred?!" Val protested. "I think the power's going to your head."

Luis had just turned twenty-one and been promoted from busboy to bartender, and he was taking his new position seriously. "Yeah, yeah. Trust me, we are going to get *slammed* tonight."

Val headed for the kitchen to get the fruit just as her mother walked over from the podium, holding a phone to her chest.

"Luis," Angela said, in a loud whisper.

"Yeah?"

"*Es la loca*, Katrine."

"Tell her I'm not here."

"She knows you're here."

"Tell her I'm dead."

Angela held the phone out. "You'd *better* talk to her. I don't want another scene."

Luis let out a big sigh and reached for the phone to talk to his ex, Katrine, aka the *muchacha loca*.

Luis and Katrine had been together from the time they were fifteen. They were supposed to get married after they graduated from college—he from St. John's with an engineering degree and she from Rutgers, premed. They hadn't set a date, but he'd bought her a ring and she'd started reading bridal magazines.

Then, out of the blue that past summer, Luis broke up with her. Everyone was shocked, especially Katrine.

She'd been making scenes ever since. Showing up at his classes at St. John's or his on-campus apartment in the middle of the night. The Saturday before this, she'd come to the restaurant at the height of the dinner rush and sat at the bar all night, holding her head in her hands, quietly crying, while all around her people drank and danced and laughed. She stayed all the way to closing, and then Pedro, Luis's father, drove her home at two in the morning.

Val backed out through the swinging kitchen door, carrying a cardboard box overflowing with tropical fruit.

"Oh, don't worry, I got it," she said to Luis as she hoisted it up onto the bar. Luis didn't notice Val's sarcasm. He was holding the phone away from his ear and wincing. Katrine's muffled lamentations echoed throughout the room.

Val looked at Carly and shook her head. "Is that who I think it is?"

Carly nodded and rolled her eyes. "Yup."

"I don't get it. Why does she keep calling?"

Carly shrugged. "I don't know." But she did know. She knew what it was like to be so obsessed you did things you knew you shouldn't. She didn't think she was as bad as Katrine. Not by a long shot. She was much more careful. She knew that you had to keep your obsession to yourself.

"See? Aren't you glad we did that intervention on you?"

Carly nodded again as she reached into the box for a pineapple.

Carly was glad it was going to be a busy night. She needed something to get her mind off the things it wanted to think about, all the questions it wanted to ponder about Taylor and Brian together, all the wondering it wanted to do about how Brian thought of Carly now, if he ever did think of her.

As Luis predicted, it was a crazy-busy night at SJNY. The line for tables in the dining room was out the door by seven. The bar was packed four deep an hour before

Los Postizos started their first set, and Luis and the other bartenders had gone through half of the three hundred fruit-laden paper umbrellas.

But the busyness of SJNY did nothing to protect Carly from her renegade brain, a brain that was a lot better at multitasking than she'd ever imagined. Now that she'd gotten her glimpse of Taylor—the face and the long, elegant neck; the smooth, shiny hair; the yogafied body and fabulous, magnanimous personality—Carly couldn't stop thinking about her. She would be taking down someone's name, the number in their party, noting their time of arrival, telling them how long they could expect to wait, and at the same time she'd see Taylor laughing it up with the Dominican girls or the firemen in Washington Square Park. When she ran back to the kitchen for two orders of flan for table ten, she'd see Taylor and her mother with the *New York Times* crossword puzzle between them. When Angela sent her to the linen closet for a pile of napkins, she wondered about the dinner at the Deen brownstone that night. Was Brian there? What were they eating? Even as she faked her way through "Happy Birthday" in Spanish, a big smile on her face, she was trying to fight off the part of her brain that wanted to know if Brian kissed Taylor the same way he had kissed her, if he touched Taylor in the same places he had touched her.

But the worst thing was what happened to her own

memories now that she knew what Taylor looked like. She tried conjuring up her favorite memory from her summer with Brian—the first night in room nine at Ernestine's when no one said, "We better stop." Now when she thought about that night—how afterward they lay side by side on Brian's futon, watching the sky change from pink and orange to deep, dark blue—she saw Taylor in her place.

It was like she'd been deleted from her own memory.

PART
two

5

SHE WASN'T always like this.

If you'd met Carly, say, just six months before, you wouldn't have pegged her as a stalker in the making. You would have found a well-behaved, reasonably confident, responsible, and by all appearances normal teenage girl living a pretty comfortable life.

Yes, her parents were divorced, but that was hardly unusual in her world. Only slightly more than half the girls at her school lived with both biological parents under one roof. (Or one of several roofs, this being the Julia Bellwin School for Girls on East 92nd Street, just off Fifth Avenue.) Slightly fewer than half shuttled back and forth across town or state or country—and in some cases, ocean.

In Carly's case, her parents' split probably improved her prospects for happiness. Anyone who knew both of them well enough—and Carly was the one person in the world who did—could see that they never would have lasted. Carly's father, Tim Finnegan, was a dedicated professor of archaeology, a man who was at his happiest sweating under the brutal sun of southwestern Turkey, where he spent six weeks every summer supervising the excavation of Aphrodisias, a once-bustling ancient Greek city named for the goddess of love. When he wasn't in the field, Tim Finnegan was quite happy to be riding his bicycle across the bucolic campus of Denman College in Greenville, Ohio, on his way to give lectures on the ancient Greek water systems and safety pins. Her mother, Isabelle Greene, was a dedicated New Yorker, a refugee from the deepest New Jersey suburbs, which she fled as an eighteen-year-old, vowing never to return. Tim and Isabelle met as graduate students at Columbia. Tim was finishing up his PhD, and Isabelle was working on a graduate degree in creative writing, hoping for a career as a novelist.

Carly's parents weren't married or even formally engaged when Isabelle became (unexpectedly but not unhappily) pregnant with Carly. But they were living together with the shared assumption that they would someday get married. The archaeology department at Columbia had an opening coming up, and Tim was considered a shoo-in when he finished his degree. So when that pink line showed up on the EPT, they went down to City Hall and exchanged vows with the happy—if vague—idea that "everything would work itself out." But then that job at Columbia went to someone else. After a three-year search, Tim was finally offered what he considered a great job: a full-time, tenure-track position at Denman. By then Isabelle was even more certain that she didn't want to live anywhere else but Manhattan—and Tim, who had put ten years of postgraduate work into preparing for his career, couldn't imagine doing anything else but archaeology. So they split.

Both of Carly's parents found new partners, and those two couples seemed, from her vantage point, better suited than the one that had produced her. Tim's second wife, Ann, was a microbiologist and epidemiologist who happily spent her husband's long absences in her lab with her microbes and pathogens.

Soon after divorcing Carly's father, her mother met and moved in with Nick, a Queens-born, self-taught sculptor specializing in large-scale installations constructed entirely out of materials found in junkyards and landfills. Nick, with his artistic aspirations and his unfinished loft in the Meatpacking District (which hadn't yet become the prime neighborhood it now was), seemed like exactly the right companion for the artsy-bohemian life Isabelle had in mind. Carly was never sure if it was because her parents' marriage failed, or because it fit her mother's idea of how an artsy-bohemian life should be lived, but Isabelle never married Nick, even after they decided to have a child together. It didn't seem to make a difference. To Carly and everyone who knew them, they seemed quite married.

Carly liked Nick. Over the years they'd developed a

close relationship. Nick never tried to be too parental with Carly. He was more like a close adult friend.

Despite the distance, Carly had a good relationship with her father and got along well with his wife, Ann. She took the short plane ride to Ohio one weekend a month to visit them. She'd spend a week or two there every summer as well as some school breaks.

Well then what about that school and those mean girls who were making fun of Val's shoes? There's a lot of pressure in those New York private schools, isn't there?

Yes, a lot of pressure. But Carly wasn't particularly susceptible to it. She went to Bellwin for free because her mother was the head of college placement. With a long record of getting Bellwin girls into top schools, Isabelle and her team of able assistants were a big part of the reason people begged, bribed, and clawed their daughters' way into the school in the first place. Though there was little in the world that her rich classmates couldn't afford, they couldn't afford to diss Isabelle Greene's daughter.

Carly wasn't one to go around wishing she could trade homes or parents or wardrobes with the rich girls at her school. She'd never minded living on the fringe of Bellwin social life. Fringe was fine with her. She had her fringe friends, Val Rivera and Paula Castleman. Though since Paula's mother married an Italian shoe magnate the year before, Paula appeared to be drifting away from the fringe to the white-hot center of Bellwin life.

Paula and Carly bonded on the first day of kindergarten, after circle-time sharing revealed them to be the only two girls in the class who had spent their entire summers in the city. No camp, no Europe, no house in "the country," wherever that was. This was back when Paula's mother managed a Madison Avenue shoe boutique and Isabelle was an assistant to the then-head of college placement. It wasn't that the five-year-olds who had summer homes and servants rejected the ones who didn't. Or that the ones who didn't—Carly and Paula—felt inferior to the ones who did. At five, Carly was more impressed by Paula's weekly trips to Coney Island than she was by Piper Peterson's week on a yacht docked in Monaco. They simply felt more comfortable with each other.

Val came to Bellwin in seventh grade, when the school was undergoing a big diversity push. Val would have gotten into Bellwin anyway. She was that smart and that disciplined. But she'd have been perfectly happy to stay at St. Cecilia's, her neighborhood Catholic school, if Bellwin hadn't found her and offered her a full scholarship.

Despite the common wisdom about three being a crowd, the three of them had managed to stay a threesome of best friends up through the end of sophomore year. She and Val were still friendly with Paula, but now they were mostly a twosome.

So how does a well-behaved, reasonably confident,

responsible, and otherwise normal teenage girl become the kind of person who spends an entire day following her ex-boyfriend's new girlfriend around the streets of Manhattan—ducking into doorways, knocking into people, and almost getting run over by taxis along the way?

It started with a string of bad luck at the end of Carly's junior year. Or what seemed like bad luck at the time. Later, at the starry-eyed height of her relationship with Brian, Carly would see the series of events that had disrupted her life as the handiwork of a celestial being, someone whose job was to bring together lovers who were destined to meet. Maybe even Aphrodite herself, the patron goddess of the ancient city Carly was supposed to spend her summer helping to unearth.

There's a picture of four-year-old Carly hanging on the wall of her father's office at Denman College. She's wearing a big floppy hat and sunglasses and peering into a shallow hole she is proud of having dug all by herself.

At first glance you might take it for a typical vacation shot. But if you stopped to study it, wondering if you knew the beach where it was taken, you'd see that the ground you took at first to be sand was reddish, densely packed dirt. You'd look in vain for a brightly colored plastic bucket by Carly's side or a glimpse of shimmering ocean behind her.

Thirteen years later, Carly could still recall the moment that picture was taken. After digging for what felt like hours but was mere minutes, she'd uncovered a trove of archaeological treasure: a clay shard, three well-worn coins, and a small metal thing she would later learn was called a fibula, a decorative pin that was to the ancient world what buttons, zippers, and Velcro are to ours.

Her father told her the shard was part of a jar or cup and at least two thousand years old. "Imagine a little girl like you, holding this in her hand," he'd said, as he placed it in hers, "drinking juice at breakfast." Carly had pictured a dark-haired girl with golden-brown skin dressed in a mini toga and sandals. She wondered whether she and the girl would like each other and what kinds of games they would play together. Up until the moment she held those things in her hand, Carly didn't get why her father was so excited about the hot, dusty place he'd dragged her and her mother to. But with this imagined playmate before her, she could finally see the city that had once been on that mountain in Turkey. At four, Carly could barely pronounce "archaeology," but now she understood why her father wanted to dig his way into those ancient lives. She wanted to dig, too.

A lot changed after that trip.

She didn't know it, but her parents had already decided to split up. In the fall her father moved to Ohio for his job. Less than a year later she and her mother moved in with Nick, and Carly grew up a city girl, surrounded by concrete and glass and asphalt and steel. But as she walked those concrete sidewalks or rode metal buses over asphalt streets, she'd always wonder what was underneath the hard surfaces, what stories were buried, waiting to be discovered. She never forgot the feeling of holding those little pieces of someone's long-ago life, and unlike most kids— who change career plans every other day—she couldn't imagine doing anything else but archaeology.

Even after she figured out that her discovery was a setup.

During her visits to Ohio, she'd spend a lot of time in her father's lab at Denman. The more she learned about archaeology in general and that dig in particular, the more suspect her discoveries seemed. It eventually dawned on her that the likelihood of finding all that stuff in the same spot was pretty low. Archaeological digs went on for years, decades even. Actual discoveries of artifacts were relatively rare. Most of the work was in the digging itself, the careful removal of layer upon layer of soil and sediment, which then had to be tested and analyzed and dated. One layer a few inches thick could represent hundreds of years. A hole a few feet deep could tell a thousand years of geological history.

When she finally asked him about it years later, Carly's father admitted that he and some of the other grad students planted the stuff for her to find.

"I wanted you to have fun. And see what it was that

took me away from home so much. I wasn't trying to make you into an archaeologist. It isn't exactly a growth industry, you know."

Oh, she knew. Carly's mother reminded her of it whenever her plan to major in archaeology came up. And Carly's father, who was still a little afraid of his ex-wife, halfheartedly tried to discourage her by telling her how boring and tedious the day-to-day work could be.

But Carly knew that nothing about archaeology bored her father.

And nothing about it—not even the slow, tedious, painstaking digging and brushing—bored her, either.

Though she hadn't been back to Aphrodisias, Carly had still managed to find archaeological opportunities in the much less ancient city of New York. She'd dug for artifacts in its junkyards and landfills with Nick, helping him find materials for his sculptures. She'd worked on the site of a colonial-era farm out in Brooklyn, where she'd touched more shards than she could count, bits of blue-and-white pottery that had belonged to the original Dutch settlers.

Something happened to her when she saw places where people lived thousands or even hundreds of years before, or touched things they touched. Whenever she visited her father's office, he would unlock the glass case her "discoveries" were kept in and let her hold them. As her finger traced the faded artwork on that shard, she could still see the little girl her imagination conjured thirteen years before. Planted or not, the shard was real, and it really was two thousand years old. Someone's robes were held together by that fibula, and those coins were passed from hand to hand in that place which once was a city.

Now she was finally going back to the place where it all started, the place where they worshipped the goddess of love. Her father, who was now in charge of the dig, had gotten a big grant, and Carly was not only going, she was going to get paid—like her father's graduate students—to clean and preserve and catalogue relics from the ancient city of Aphrodisias.

Carly's bags weren't exactly packed when he called three weeks before they were scheduled to leave, but they might as well have been. The trip was pretty much all she was thinking about in between studying for exams. In fact the call came when she was at a camping-equipment store downtown. Her father had sent her a gift card and made her promise to buy clothes with the official seal of approval from the American Dermatological Society.

"The sun over there is brutal. I promised your mother we'd be careful." She'd managed to find a not-too-ugly, dermatologist-approved, long-sleeved shirt with UVA and UVB protection, and she was heading over to check out dermatologist-approved hats. When her phone rang and DAD flashed on the screen, she assumed he was calling to remind her of something else she needed to pack or do for the trip. Did she have the right shoes? Good sunscreen? A sun hat? Layers for night when the desert gets surprisingly cold? "Feminine products," because they were sometimes hard to find in the villages near the dig? Was she sure her passport was valid? Had she gotten her gamma globulin shot, was her tetanus up to date?

She answered the call with: "I got SPF nine hundred ninety-nine, and I'm bringing three hundred tampons, so you can stop torturing yourself."

"Carly, it's Dad."

"Yeah, Dad, I know. You think that's how I answer the phone for everyone?"

"Oh." He made a noise approximating laughter. "Of course. Sorry. Listen—I'm afraid I've got some bad news. No. Wait. What am I saying? It's—" The connection started to break up. It sounded like her father had just jumped into a swimming pool. "—news, in fact."

"Wait a sec. I barely have a signal here." She hung the shirt from a shelf full of PowerBars and headed toward the exit. Something about her father's tone told her she wouldn't be coming back for it.

As soon she set foot on the sidewalk, he said, "Ann's pregnant."

"Oh." It was late afternoon on a warm Saturday in spring. The first truly warm, summer's-just-around-the-corner Saturday, and Broadway was thick with shoppers.

For three years, Carly's father and his wife had been trying desperately to have a baby, using everything science had to offer. Ann had gotten pregnant twice through in vitro fertilization but had miscarriages both times. The last Carly had heard, they were going to give the test-tube method one more try before starting the adoption process. But not until after the summer.

"I thought you guys had decided to wait until we got back before you—"

"Did the next round of IVF, I know. That's what's so crazy! This just happened. The old-fashioned, low-tech way."

"Oh."

"Nature took its course."

"Uh-huh."

"We really didn't think it was possible. Ann threw away her diaphragm a long time ago—"

"Dad."

"And if you don't *have* to use a condom, then—"

"Dad—"

"God, when I think of all the trouble we've been through. The money we've spent. Did you know we were spinning my sperm to make it more concentrated?"

"Dad! Please—you can spare me the details."

"Oh. Sorry. It's just—I'm excited."

Carly already knew way more about their procreative

woes than she needed or cared to know. One morning during her winter break visit two years earlier she had awakened to her father calling up the stairs to say, "We're going to get Ann inseminated."

After they left, she made the mistake of flipping through a brochure from the Center for Reproductive Health, which explained all about sperm collection. For days she was tormented by thoughts of her father entering a little room with a DVD player full of porn—actually, the brochure used the term "erotic materials"—holding a little plastic cup.

"So I guess this means—"

Her father sighed into his phone, sending a crackly static into her ear. "Yeah. That's the bad-news part. I'm really sorry. Ann said I should go. That there's nothing I can do here, and with the grant and everything . . . She's already at sixteen weeks, and the doctor thinks we can breathe easy since the miscarriages were both at eight weeks—"

"Sixteen weeks? That's four months!? And you're telling me now?"

"I know. It's crazy, but we didn't realize it ourselves until two weeks ago. Ann's cycle's been off since the fertility treatments, which also made her gain weight."

"Mm-hmm."

"We'll go next summer. I promise. No matter what."

"Mm-hmm."

"Listen. Ann and I were talking, and we have an idea. Why don't you come out here for the summer?"

"To *Greenville?*"

"Yes, Carly, to Greenville. You say it like it's Mars. It's really a great place to be in summer. I'll pay you to be my research assistant. We can still get a lot done even if we're not at the site."

"Like what?"

"I've got findings that need writing up. There's correspondence. You could take a summer-school class, get to know the campus from a student's point of view."

Greenville, Ohio, population 3,167, home to Denman College, was the last place Carly wanted to spend the summer. Holidays and school vacations were boring enough. But in a little over a year she'd be moving there to start her freshman year at Denman, where as the child of a faculty member, she would get free tuition and was pretty much guaranteed admission.

Before he and Ann bought their house and spent something like fifty thousand dollars trying to get Ann pregnant, Carly's going to Denman had been talked about as a "possibility," a backup plan if there wasn't enough money for her to go elsewhere. But now, if she was going to college—and neither of her academic-professional parents could so much as imagine she wouldn't—she was going to Denman.

Denman was a perfectly fine school. And if it had been

on one of the coasts, or closer to a real city (Columbus didn't count), or if her father didn't teach there, she might have been interested. It did have a good, if small, archaeology department.

But it was surrounded by cornfields.

And Amish people who sometimes drove their horse-drawn buggies into town.

And the one friend Carly had in that town, Jolie Albright, who lived next door to her father and Ann, had not only become a meth-head, she'd robbed a 7-Eleven and gone to Juvie. (Which, Jolie's mother had confided to Carly on her last visit, Jolie's parents were actually glad about because they figured she might at least get clean that way.)

No way Carly was spending any more time in Greenville than she absolutely had to.

6

AN HOUR after that conversation with her father, Carly and Val sat at the SJNY bar, contemplating life's injustices.

"How far along is she?" Val asked.

"Sixteen weeks."

"Sixteen weeks? And he's just telling you now?"

"I know. I hate that baby. Or embryo or whatever it is."

"Fetus."

"What?"

"First it's a zygote. Then it's a blastocyst. After it makes its way down the fallopian tube it's an embryo. After eight weeks, it's a fetus."

A year had passed since Val aced the AP Bio exam, and she still had that stuff down. If anyone was ever destined to be a doctor, she was.

"And you don't hate it."

"Yeah. I do. I've waited years for this trip. *Years.*"

"You can't hold that against the kid."

"Wanna bet?" Carly knew she wouldn't, though, not once it was here. "And no way am I going there for the summer."

"Of course not. But what are you going to do?"

Carly shrugged. "Maybe volunteer at the Brooklyn dig again."

"Okay. Good. And you'll work here nights."

"Is your mother okay with that?"

"She will be. Hey, *mamá*—" Val's mother was standing at a podium by the front door, going over the night's reservations with Val's uncle, Pedro. "Can Carly work here this summer?"

"I thought she was going to Greece."

"Turkey," Carly said. "The part that used to be Greece." Like it mattered. "But now I'm not going anyway."

"Why not? You were so excited."

Val launched into rapid Spanish that, from the way Angela ran over to the bar and hugged her, Carly gathered contained her father's news.

"You can work all the hours you need. Maybe even let you wait tables." Angela clicked her way back to the podium.

There was good money to be made waiting tables. Val said waiters and waitresses made two hundred dollars some nights.

"We could indulge ourselves a little," Val said. "Maybe go to some shows. Some nice restaurants."

- - -

In the grand scheme of things, having your fabulous summer plans canceled for reasons beyond your control isn't exactly tragic. Carly didn't doubt her father's promise to take her the following year. He wasn't one of those fathers who went around making promises he couldn't or wouldn't keep. She knew she'd get there. And she didn't really have any objections to a new sibling. She already had Jess. And Jess wasn't bad. Kind of cool, actually. Her seven-year-old company was preferable to the company of many seventeen-year-olds.

Carly was sorry to lose the bragging rights, though. She'd no longer be able to say "I'm going on an archaeological dig in Turkey," instead of "nothing" in the annual can-you-top-this buzz about fabulous summer plans at the Julia Bellwin School for Girls. For once she had been able to compete with her classmates' internships at French *Vogue*, their sailing camps off the coast of Maine, their service trips to Guatemala (followed by recovery at a spa in Mexico). But she'd live.

She was disappointed about not going to Turkey. Very disappointed. But by the end of the night she'd started getting used to the idea of staying in the city for the summer. She and Val always had fun together. She could check out the Brooklyn dig.

College kids from all over the country headed to New

York in the summer. People from all over the world came here.

So she was staying home in New York. There were worse things.

But soon after Carly absorbed her father's news she got more bad news from her mother, news that would change everything.

Carly spent that night at Val's, like she did whenever she worked late. The next morning, she called her mother to tell her about Ann's pregnancy and the canceled trip.

After a strange silence, Isabelle said, "Well, that's crap timing for us."

"For us?"

"I mean for you. I know how much you were looking forward to the trip."

"Yeah. Well, Dad says we'll go next year."

"Uh-huh."

Carly thought her mother sounded weird. Like she had something to say but wasn't saying it.

"Get this—he wants me to go there for the summer."

When Carly heard her mother say "Might not be a bad idea," she knew for sure that something was going on.

"What? This from Ms. Give Me Manhattan or Give Me Death?"

"Listen, Carly. I also have some news."

"Don't tell me you're pregnant, too."

Judging by the dead air on the other end of the phone, Isabelle didn't find that funny.

"Can you meet me down here so we can talk in person?"

Carly's mother often spent Sunday mornings in her office at Bellwin. She said she never got anything done during the regular school day, when she had back-to-back meetings and endless phone conversations with anxious parents, obsessed students, and admissions people. On Sundays she could get the quiet she needed for all the detail work—writing letters, reviewing applications—that went into her job.

When Carly arrived, Isabelle wasted no time getting her news out. After thirteen years and a child though no official marriage, she and Nick were splitting up.

Carly knew they'd had been having problems during the past year. She'd heard the fights, and the silence between them that often followed the fights. She didn't understand it all, but she thought it had to do with careers and money.

On the surface things were good. Nick was starting to have some serious success as an artist. Museums were buying his giant, room-sized installations. Collectors were buying the smaller, individual sculptures. He'd even had a piece in a show at the Museum of Modern Art the year before.

Isabelle had plenty of success, too. But it wasn't the kind of success she wanted. Working at Bellwin was never supposed to be a career. It was supposed to be a day job, the thing she did until she could make a living as a writer. But over the years, the day job turned into a day, night, and weekend job. Writing time was squeezed into summers. Once Jess came along, it got even harder for Isabelle to find time to write, and impossible to even think of quitting. The job came with free tuition for her daughters—and in New York, where the good public schools are almost as hard to get into as the private ones, this was huge.

In one of the fights Carly overheard, Nick offered to support Isabelle while she took time off to write. He said he'd pay tuition for both girls, but she wouldn't let him. She said things were already uneven enough since he owned the loft. Plus she was so out of practice. And there were so many good, younger writers.

But that spring things had quieted down, and Carly took the quiet to mean Nick and her mother were working things out. She'd been babysitting for Jess on Monday nights while they went to see a counselor. And on one of those Monday nights after putting Jess to bed, Carly had accidentally walked in on Nick and Isabelle making out. She hadn't heard them come home when she wandered into the dark kitchen looking for something to eat.

She flipped on the light to find her mother up against the counter with her blouse half unbuttoned and Nick awkwardly adjusting his pants.

It was beyond embarrassing but at the same time reassuring. Carly thought it meant things were going to be okay. If they couldn't keep their hands off each other until they got to the bedroom, that had to mean something, right?

Plus hadn't they gone away together just a few weeks before?

When she got to her mother's office, Carly asked about that weekend getaway.

"Oh. Honey, that wasn't a romantic thing," Isabelle explained as she flipped through a pile of folders on her desk. "We went out of town so we could finally decide once and for all. We hashed it out and decided we were done. And now that we've decided, there's no point in fighting."

"But that was weeks ago," Carly said, trying to get her mother to look at her. But Isabelle wouldn't look up from her desk.

"We agreed to wait until the school year ended before taking any action." She picked up the folders and rolled her chair over to the filing cabinet next to her desk. She placed the folders in the long drawer, closed it, and locked it.

"Mom, you're acting like this is no big deal. Like you didn't just spend thirteen years with this person. Aren't you upset? Aren't you sad? Is this what you want?"

Now Carly had her mother's attention. Isabelle looked up her daughter. A hint of a tear glistened on the surface of one eye but then disappeared without falling.

"The question isn't what I want, Carly. It's just what is. I have to accept it. And move forward. Come on, let's get out of here. We'll take a cab. I'm too tired for the subway."

Carly spent the whole cab ride staring out the window, wondering how she'd managed not to notice this pretty major thing happening right in front of her. Sure, she hadn't seen them together a lot in the past month. But that wasn't so unusual. Nick had a show coming up and was putting in long hours in his studio. He did that sometimes when he was under a deadline or caught up in an inspiration. He'd work through the night, taking power naps on the futon he kept in there.

Isabelle seemed to be her usual busy self, dealing with the last of the wait-listers, meeting with next year's crop of demanding parents. She'd been spending a lot of time in her room reading, but Carly hadn't thought much of it. She figured it was just the usual end-of-the-school-year exhaustion.

"Now I have to figure out the living situation."

"The living situation?"

Carly turned to look at her mother but she was staring out the other cab window.

"The loft is Nick's. We're going to have to leave."

When Carly and her mother moved in with Nick twelve years earlier, the Meatpacking District was still a place where they processed animals into meat, not the locale of hot clubs and designer boutiques. Nick's huge loft was nothing but unfinished industrial space that still smelled slightly of the veal factory it once housed. There were no walls, no adequate heat, and not much in the way of plumbing except an old toilet and sink surrounded by plywood and a bathtub in the middle of the "kitchen," which consisted of a hotplate and a microwave.

It took four years and a lot of sweat to turn it into the huge, light-filled space it now was—with high ceilings, hardwood floors, and a kitchen with all the latest appliances.

Though she'd never want to go back to those conditions, Carly looked back happily on the years of roughing it. Isabelle had her assistant's job at Bellwin, but she kept a little desk set up in a corner of Nick's studio, where she wrote at night and on the weekends. They had a circle of artist and writer friends who would come over for big, loud spaghetti dinners where the talking and laughing would last late into the night.

Nick worked nights tending bar and during the day worked on the loft renovations. So that they wouldn't have to spend money on preschool, Carly stayed home with Nick while her mother worked. When other kids her age were gluing together popsicle-stick houses, she was sanding floors, installing drywall, and laying tile. Of course she mostly watched while Nick and a few hired guys did most of the real work, but Nick had always made her feel like she was a part of things. She'd fetch their tools, hold the measuring tape, vacuum sawdust.

Nick let her pick out the exact spot along the wall of windows where she liked the view the best and then built her room around it. From her bed she could see across the Hudson to Jersey City or watch the cruise ships and tour boats come and go in the harbor. She'd spent many hours of her life looking out at that view, losing herself in daydreams. Girls at school were always impressed with Carly's address and the size of the loft. While it was nice to have a lot of space and a great view, for Carly it was never about status. It was about having a place where she belonged and that belonged to her.

The loft was home.

"Can't we get a place here?" As Carly said this to her mother, the cab pulled up in front of their building. Their new neighbors, a German supermodel whose face had been on the cover of *Vogue* a month earlier and the famous French photographer who took the picture, emerged and signaled for the driver to wait.

Their clothes probably cost more than Carly's mother could afford for a month's rent. There wasn't a unit in the building worth less than two million dollars, and the block was lined with galleries and designer clothing stores.

Isabelle didn't bother answering the question, and Carly

didn't bother repeating it as they passed Gudrun and Jean-François, who nodded solemnly—or was it smugly?—while holding the cab door.

"The rental market is even worse than I thought," Isabelle said, turning her key in the wall-mounted locking system.

The door clicked and buzzed. Carly pushed it open.

"I haven't been able to find anything—anywhere in Manhattan—that we can afford with even half the space we'll need."

The lobby still looked like it had when they moved in twelve years before—except for the row of locked mailboxes along the back wall. The cracks and holes in the concrete floor hadn't been filled, and no one had even tried to remove the graffiti. Carly used to wonder about that until she decided that people who could afford to live there liked it that way. It gave them the illusion of living on the edge.

She pushed the elevator button. Her mother leaned against the wall like she needed the support. Isabelle looked tired. More tired than usual. The circles under her eyes were showing despite the chalky-pink concealer.

"You've already been looking for apartments?" Carly had to shout over the elevator's clanking descent toward the lobby.

"This is not a sudden decision. Believe me."

"But why didn't you tell me? Give me some inkling?"

"I didn't want to ruin your summer. I knew how much

you were looking forward to that time with your father. I figured I'd find a place and get us all moved in while you were away."

The elevator landed with a *thud*. Carly pulled the folding metal gate open. The industrial elevator was another leftover from the veal factory. Wide enough for a rolling rack of calf carcasses, its linoleum floor was stained brown with blood and who knew what else.

"You were just going to spring it on me when I landed at JFK? Bring me home to some strange place, not even let me pack my own stuff?"

Isabelle leaned against the graffiti-covered wall and let out one of her trademark groan-sighs. "You know, Carly, I really haven't thought it all through. I'm kind of going by the seat of my pants here."

Carly pulled the gate closed. "So what happens next?"

"That's the other thing I need to tell you."

The ride to the sixth floor was slow enough for Isabelle to tell Carly all about the "great opportunity" that had presented itself. Old friends of Isabelle's sister, Nancy, owned a summer camp on a lake outside New Paltz. Their director had been in a rock-climbing accident the week before, and they needed someone who could step in and run the place for the summer.

Isabelle had convinced herself that filling in as director would solve all the problems.

"One, it gives me a place to stay for the time being, while I keep looking for an apartment. Two, I need the money. I'm going to need a security deposit and broker's fee. And three, Jess can go to camp for free, which'll be just what she needs this summer."

"Does Jess even *know*?"

"Not yet. We're waiting for the right time."

Before Carly had a chance to ask what her mother meant by "right time," the elevator opened into the middle of Nick's studio. The air was thick with the acrid smell of burning metal, and the Ramones were blasting through the room. When Nick had a deadline, he'd play old-school punk on a nonstop loop. Jess stood off to the side in kid-sized safety goggles and grease-smeared apron, watching her father weld.

The goggles and apron used to be Carly's.

Carly never knew how to refer to Nick with other people. "My mother's boyfriend" made him sound inconsequential, like someone passing through her life. Isabelle sometimes used "partner" when she talked about Nick to other people, but Carly thought that sounded ridiculous, like they were accountants or lawyers. She'd settled on not explaining and just called him her stepfather.

Now what was she supposed to call him, her ex-stepfather? Her sister's father? Her mother's ex? What kind of relationship would they have after Carly moved away?

As soon as she saw them, Jess ran over and threw her

arms around her mother's waist. Isabelle hugged Jess, leaned down to kiss the top of her head and didn't let go until Jess's loud but muffled "I can't breathe!"

Squirming out from under her mother's arms, Jess pointed to a rusted bicycle wheel on the floor next to Nick. Various random metal things had been soldered to it: a fork, a spoon, a shiny sheriff's badge.

"Look at my sculpture!"

With a weak smile Isabelle said, "Nice, honey," and headed for the door to the living part of the loft.

Nick didn't turn off the blowtorch or lift his goggles. He just waved in their general direction as they walked through the studio. Isabelle made a motion with her hand that somewhat resembled a wave back.

As they walked, Carly told her mother about her plan to work at SJNY for the summer and volunteer at the dig in Brooklyn.

"And stay where?"

"Can't I stay here?"

Isabelle shook her head.

"Why not? Nick isn't kicking us out, is he?"

"No. No. I'm sure it would be fine with him. It's just— not a good idea." Isabelle tossed her keys into the bowl on the counter between the kitchen and dining room, then continued down the hall to her and Nick's bedroom.

"Why not?"

"I need a clean break. Or as clean as possible considering

we have Jess. If you stay here while I'm away, it'll just complicate things further." She opened her closet door, kicked off her shoes, and stepped into her slippers.

"How? I don't understand."

Groan-sigh. "Because if you're here, and I'm there, it'll mean that Nick and I will have to talk about you and what you're doing and I—I'm just not up for that right now. I want to work on healing, and I won't be able to do that if I have to talk to him all the time."

"Yeah, but aren't you guys going to have to talk about Jess anyway?"

"We've already worked out the summer, so not really. He'll come up to see Jess during the parents' weekends. I don't need to add you to the mix."

"What does that mean, 'add me to the mix'? What would you even need to talk about? I'm responsible; I can take care of myself. I totally *do* take care of myself now."

"Carly, this isn't open for discussion. You're not eighteen yet, and I'm not going to let you run wild around the city. I've seen enough of that with the girls at Bellwin. You can go to your father's, or, if you want I can probably get you a job at Stony Hollow. Though I'm not sure what jobs are left at this late date."

"But—"

"Carly. I can't talk about this right now. Can you understand? I'm just—I'm just exhausted. And I feel a migraine coming on. I need to get in bed."

"What about dinner?"

"Could you order pizza? And see that Jess gets to bed at a decent hour? Nick's in one of those oblivious-to-time-and-responsibility states."

"I guess."

"And please make sure she has a clean uniform for tomorrow?"

Carly let out a groan-sigh of her own. "Okay."

"Thanks, honey. Really. I appreciate your help. I know this is has all got to be a shock. First your father flakes on you—"

"Mom—he's having a baby. I wouldn't exactly call that flaking."

"No. Of course not. I just mean that's how it must feel. It's something you've been looking forward to for so long."

Like losing the only home she'd known for the past twelve years was nothing, just an incidental change of scene.

7

"WHY'S EVERYBODY so crabby?" Jess was gouging a piece of spinach out of her pizza with her finger. Her paper plate was dotted with dark green blobs of oily spinach she'd extracted, one by one.

The question hung there in the air above the worktable in Nick's studio. Carly looked across at Nick, who looked down at his pizza. It was a veggie special from Salvatore's. Nick and Carly's favorite.

The two of them became vegetarians together one boiling hot day in the summer after she and her mother moved into the loft. They were walking by a warehouse just as a truck full of carcasses was being unloaded. Even though they were headless and hoofless and cut in half, they still looked more like animals than food as they hung from those giant hooks. And they were small. It would be a few months before Carly would be able to make out the writing on the side of the truck, but the smiling creature underneath "Valenzano's Veal" with its big black happy eyes was clearly just a baby, and no way would it be smiling if it knew what was inside the truck.

One of the workers greeted Carly with a wink and a smile and a "Hey, sweetheart" as he hoisted one of the carcasses—a leg in each hand—onto a cart.

It was a strange experience for Carly, who was five at the time and in love with animals. The man seemed so nice. And yet he was swinging this dead animal around like it was nothing. Like it had never been anything.

She knew what "meatpacking" meant. She knew there were still working warehouses around. She'd been breathing in the tinny smell of blood and the stink of garbage trucks that collected the rotting discards, since moving in. But seeing that calf in that guy's hands sent her over the edge, and Carly declared she would never again eat an animal.

Isabelle, concerned about protein, tried to convince Carly to keep chicken or at least fish in her diet. But not eating animals didn't feel like a choice to Carly. Nick had been there. He'd seen how that dead calf had affected Carly, and he took her side. He said he didn't mind cooking and eating vegetarian. It would be healthier, anyway. So from that day on, they were a mostly meatless (almost) family.

Carly hadn't had a chance to talk to Nick alone since her mother dropped her news bomb, but they knew each other too well. From the guilty way he was avoiding eye contact, it was clear he knew that she knew.

When neither of them answered, Jess tried again. "Why's everyone in a bad mood?"

"*I'm* not in a bad mood," Carly said.

"Yes, you are. You're not talking. Daddy's not talking. Mama went to bed while it was still light out."

"Your mother has a headache, Jess," Nick said. "And I have this show coming up. I'm sorry I've been distracted."

He looked up at Carly, like he was hoping for some help. But Carly didn't offer any. She wasn't going to take matters into her own hands and tell Jess herself, but she wasn't going to pretend everything was just fine, either. She didn't understand why Nick and her mother thought delaying the news was going to make it any easier for Jess. If anything, Carly thought, it was going to make things worse.

When it was clear that Carly wasn't going to help, Nick reverted to the foolproof Jess-distracting method. "So tell us about the play."

Jess was a budding playwright. She and her friend Rosie were hard at work on an original script for their second-grade class.

"Well," she said, homing in on an errant artichoke. "It's about these girls. Actually they're princesses who are on an adventure. They were kidnapped by these witches, but they escape and they have to find their way back to their castle before their father dies of sadness. See, his wife— their mother—died already, and now his daughters have been taken, and he's just too sad."

"Wow. That does sound sad," Carly said. Maybe Jess knew more than everyone thought. "What happened to their mother?"

"Oh, she had a heart attack because she ate too many french fries from McDonald's."

Carly laughed, relieved that the sad queen bore no resemblance to their mother. "They have McDonald's in this kingdom?"

"Yeah. Well, we call it Ye Olde Royal McDonald's, but it's basically the same thing. Too much fat. And stress. She was very stressed."

"Really? I didn't think queens had that much stress in their lives. 'Cause of all the servants and stuff."

"Yeah, well, that's what the stress was all about. Her servants were a lot to manage. And she was just—stressed. See, we're trying to put in some positive messages."

"Maybe she should have done yoga."

"They didn't have yoga back then."

"But they had McDonald's."

"Yes. They did. In our version of back then, they did. We're using our poetic licenses, okay? Do you think maybe you could just listen and not keep interrupting?"

- - -

As soon as Carly put Jess to bed, she went back to Nick's studio. The music was blaring and the blowtorch burning again. He was welding a spiraled spool of metal, which looked something like a thick, rusty Slinky, along the edge of a large metal box. He held up a finger to tell Carly he'd stop in a minute.

She sat down on his wheeled stool to wait. She used to spin herself dizzy on that thing, or lie on her stomach and push herself across the length of the room as fast as she could. Once she'd smashed into the wall headfirst and gotten a huge bump on the top of her skull. She and Nick decided they wouldn't tell Isabelle because she'd make Carly stop riding the stool, or want her to wear a helmet or something. They agreed they'd just be a lot more careful from then on.

That's how they invented the DTM code for "Don't tell Mom." They never did it for really big stuff, but for the little things, where telling would serve no purpose except to get Isabelle all worked up. Like the time Carly skinned her knee when she and Nick were hunting at one of their favorite junkyards. At the time, Isabelle didn't even know Nick sometimes took her along on his junkyard jaunts, so that was an obvious DTM. They attributed the bloody knee to a fall in the park.

"Hey," Nick said, as he walked across the room.

Carly got right to it. "Mom told me."

Nick took off the goggles and gloves, wiped the sweat from his forehead, and sat down on the wooden bench across from the stool.

"I gathered."

"I can't believe I'm not going to live here anymore."

"Me neither." He reached for a coffee mug on the table behind him. From the look of it—a skin of cream floated on top—it had been there for a while. "I wish your mother would reconsider my idea."

"What idea?"

Five minutes later Carly burst into her mother's room without knocking.

"Carly, geez. You scared me."

Good, Carly thought. She wanted her mother's attention. She plopped herself down on the edge of the bed. The book Isabelle had been reading fell to her side. *Families Apart: Ten Keys to Successful Co-Parenting.* Next to it was *Mom's House, Dad's House: Making Two Homes for Your Child* and next to that, *The Good Divorce.*

"Why are we moving when Nick says we can stay?"

Isabelle had left some key information out of her version of events. Like the part about how Nick said they could stay in the loft. *Wanted* them to stay in the loft. He'd drawn up a brilliant floor plan that involved knocking down walls and building new ones to split the space into two apartments. The girls' rooms would be in the middle, with one door leading into Isabelle's (hypothetical) apartment and another leading into Nick's. There'd be no need for them to move, no need to schlep Jess back and forth for half of every week or every other week or whatever they were planning. Nick would charge Isabelle rent—because she was like that, and he knew she'd never agree otherwise—but no more than she could afford, and nothing close to what he could get for the place on the open market.

And he and Carly wouldn't have to figure out how to carry on an ex-almost-stepfather/ex-almost-stepdaughter relationship. They'd just see each other whenever. She wouldn't have to worry about what to call him. They would still be connected.

But Isabelle turned Nick down flat, and Carly wanted to know why.

"I don't want to live like that."

"Live like what?"

"Apart but together. Together but apart. You're old enough to imagine, aren't you, how hard that would be for me? I don't want to come home and smell his dinner cooking, or hear his music through the walls. Or that wo—another woman's voice."

"Is that why you guys are breaking up?"

Isabelle looked down at the bed and fingered the frayed edge of the comforter cover.

"Oh my God. Is that it? Is Nick having—" Was it still

an "affair" if you weren't married to begin with?

Isabelle reached across the bed and took Carly's hand. "It's not what you think. Yes. He's seeing someone. But that's not the reason we're breaking up. I've known about it. We both—"

"Oh my God, Mom. Stop." Carly yanked her hand away and put both hands up to her ears. This was worse than listening to her father explain the mechanics of getting Ann pregnant. "I don't want to hear it. Whatever it is."

Actually, Carly's mind was racing with questions. But they were questions she didn't want the answers to. Were they *both* "seeing" other people? Of all the stupid euphemisms, that had to be one of the stupidest. Is that why they never actually married? Was that part of the deal all along? Who would Isabelle be "seeing"? And when? Those Sundays in her office? *In* her office? On the couch under the portrait of virginal (so everyone assumed) Julia Bellwin herself?

If it weren't her life—if it weren't her mother and her about-to-be-ex-almost-stepfather and there weren't a seven-year-old involved then, Carly thought, it might be funny.

"I'm sorry. You're right. I shouldn't burden you with our stuff. Listen, I wish I were the kind of person who could do what Nick's proposing. It sounds very—European and sophisticated. Everyone thinks I'm nuts for turning him down." Isabelle shrugged and shook her head. "Sometimes *I* think I'm nuts for turning him down. But I think it would be confusing for Jess. And . . . I know myself. I won't be able to build a new life with Nick on the other side of the wall."

"But you said yourself it's a crazy market. Where are we going to go?"

"I'll find something. I know I will. But I—"

Carly cut her off. "You aren't the only one affected here. What about Jess? What about me? Nick wants us to stay. I want to stay. Jess would want to stay if she had any idea of what was going on. You're going to ruin everyone's life because you changed your mind and decided that your open marriage wasn't so cool anymore?"

Carly was glad to see Isabelle flinch. She wanted to inflict pain. She wanted a fight.

But Isabelle wouldn't bite. "I'm going to ignore that. I'm not going to try to explain my choices to you. But you've just heard some very upsetting news, and I don't blame you for lashing out."

Carly wished Isabelle would blame her. She wanted her mother to yell so that she could yell back. She wanted to scream, to throw something, to see mother flinch again.

Carly called Val to discuss.

"I vote for the camp," said Val.

"Really? I thought you'd say Ohio."

"Nah. Camp."

"Why?"

"For one, it's only a two-hour train ride away, and you can come down to the city on your days off."

"And you can come up."

"Maybe. I don't know. I don't like woods."

"Okay. What else?"

"Counselors. Have you seen this camp's Web site?"

"No."

"I'm looking at it right now. The tennis guy is hot. He goes to Georgetown. And there's a swimming instructor. Ray Booker. Amherst. And wow. I mean *wow*!"

"But we hate guys like that."

"Correction. You hate guys like that. I'm reevaluating my position."

"Jake?" Jake Alden, a senior at Edward G. Champion, was Val's lab partner in AP physics. (EGC and Bellwin offered some specialized classes jointly.) For a year, Carly had been hearing the ongoing narrative of this contentious pair. They were both supersmart, both bent on med school, and neither quite trusted the other to do things right. But over the course of the school year, aversion had morphed into attraction, just like in the movies.

And just like in the movies, there were obstacles. Jake's long-term girlfriend, Juliet Kinkade, for one, and his rich, Social-Registered family for another. The last Carly had heard, Juliet was out of the picture and Jake was calling, but Val was still insisting that she didn't want to have anything to do with "a guy like that," meaning a guy whose ancestors came over on the *Mayflower* and whose family name was on multiple buildings on multiple college campuses. Not that Jake had done or said anything to indicate that he looked down on Val or that his family would object to her. He'd even come in to SJNY for dinner with his mother, and she was totally nice to Val. Carly had been urging Val to give him a chance, to at least let herself have some fun. But Val was stubborn and laser-focused when it came to her future. She'd kept all boys—not just Jake—at a distance. She said she was saving herself. Not for marriage but until she was safely enrolled in college.

"Yeah. He called again tonight and pretty much begged me to go to the formal."

"You're kidding."

"Nope."

"Wow." The EGC senior formal was another one of those things—like summers in Paris—that belonged to the world of Piper Petersons and Celine Hardimans. Carly and Val had always tuned out when talk of the designer dresses and before-and-after parties started in April.

"And you said . . . ?"

"Yes. Believe it or not, I said yes. He was so sweet about it. I couldn't say anything else."

"Wow. That's great." Carly really did think it was great. From what Val had told her, Jake sounded like a nice guy. So what if he was rich? "It took you two long enough."

"I know."

At the time, it didn't occur to Carly to think of Val's announcement as anything but good news.

Carly must have slept some, but it felt like she was awake the whole night trying to decide between two awful options. She heard the party girls' heels click their way down the street when the bars closed at three and the rumbling of trucks outside the one meat plant still in operation at about five.

When she got up at six, she'd made up her mind.

Val made some good points. Under different circumstances, she probably would have chosen the camp over Ohio, but she was too mad at her mother for ruining her life and couldn't imagine going anywhere with her. And so that afternoon, she called her father.

"That's great. You could really be a help around here, too, now that Ann's on bedrest."

"Bedrest?"

Just that morning, Ann had experienced some bleeding and cramping. Because of the two prior miscarriages, she'd been advised to get into bed until further notice.

Carly pictured herself carrying trays of food into Ann's

room, watching Oprah in the afternoons. Suddenly she understood Jolie Albright. Who *wouldn't* start holding up 7-Elevens under those circumstances?

And so Stony Hollow it was. The only job left by then was kitchen assistant, but that was fine with Carly. She wasn't the counselor type. As much as she loved Jess, she didn't see herself spending twenty-four hours a day in the company of ten girls Jess's age.

8

GETTING OUT of New York was a depressing, exhausting experience, starting with the scene in front of what was about to become her former home.

Nick and Isabelle were being all fake-polite to each other as they loaded the cab.

"Let me get that."

"Thanks."

"You sure you don't want me to come to the station with you? Help with your luggage?"

Isabelle was nothing if not organized. She had sent most of their stuff ahead. All they had to carry was a small rolling carry-on each.

"Positive. Really. We'll be fine, won't we, girls?"

They were saying all the right, *let's-be-civil-about-this* things but avoiding eye contact as they said them. As soon as the bags were in the trunk, Isabelle climbed into the backseat without another word to Nick, who was focused on Jess, who was finally reacting to the news that her parents were splitting up. She was crying and clinging to her

father, saying, "I don't want to go, I don't want to go. I
want to stay here, with you."

Isabelle and Nick had waited until a week before to
tell her, and when they had, they'd shown her the full-
color brochure from Stony Hollow, open to the page with
the picture of a girl her age, smiling from the saddle of a
pretty white horse, wearing a nifty velvet riding helmet.

*Hey, yeah. So your parents are calling it quits, but don't
worry, kid, 'cause you get to spend the summer on top of
Snowflake here!*

The distraction tactic seemed to work. But then all that
week Jess had watched as Carly and her mother packed
up the entire contents of their rooms into boxes. They
still didn't have a place. The plan was for Isabelle to keep
looking by Web and phone, and when she got something,
Nick would move them in. Jess didn't have to do any packing. Her room at Nick's would stay unchanged, and they'd
get new stuff for her mother's place. This, along with the
pretty horses, was somehow supposed to soften the blow.

But it was clear to Carly as she stood on the sidewalk
watching all this that rainy morning, with the cab meter
running and the cabbie repeatedly checking his watch,
that Nick and Isabelle had only delayed the blow, possibly
even made it worse.

Nick squatted down to Jess's level and took her hands
in his. He promised to talk to her every day, to come and
visit as soon as possible.

But she was having none of it. She pulled her hands out of his grip and threw herself on him—wrapped her arms and legs around him with such force that he almost fell over. If there hadn't been a parking meter for Nick to grab on to, they would have both wound up on the sidewalk.

Her mother asked Carly to get Jess off Nick, but Carly refused, and in the end her mom had to get back out of the cab and peel Jess off Nick herself. Jess still wouldn't give up. It took the two of them to get her into the cab and strap her into her seat belt.

Once Jess was strapped in, Nick tried to engage Carly in a meaningful good-bye. But that would have required that she look him in the eye, and this wasn't something she was ready to do. She didn't know what she was supposed to say to him. She didn't know how she felt about him anymore, either. She believed her mother when she said that he wasn't to blame, that it was more complicated. She had no idea if "seeing someone" meant a big love thing or something more casual. And she didn't want to know. But it creeped her out to think that he had a secret life, even if it was a secret he shared with Isabelle, and even if Isabelle had one, too. When she'd first heard her mother's plan, she'd worried about him, imagining him rattling around the empty loft with no one to talk to. Apparently Nick would be just fine.

"So you'll call me?" he asked.

She shrugged and kept her eyes on the sidewalk.

"Is it okay if I call you?"

"I guess," she said, still not looking up.

"You'll keep an eye on Jess?"

"Yes," she said, and escaped into the cab.

When they finally got to Penn Station, Isabelle blew up at the ticket guy when he told her that their reservations were for the next day. It wasn't a big deal—there was still plenty of room on that day's train—but that didn't stop her from berating him, the unidentified person who had messed up her reservation, the entire Amtrak organization, and the United States of America, for selling its soul to the airline and automobile industries and settling for the "train system of a third-world country."

Jess fell into a deep, posttantrum sleep as soon as they pulled out of the station. Isabelle mostly stared out the window, every now and then reading a page or two in the book on her lap, *Basic Camp Management*. Then she'd give up with a groan-sigh and stare out the window again.

9

CARLY SHOULD have known better.

She should have taken one look at Cameron Foster with his wispy blond hair and his puka beads and Top-Siders and run the other way. But the scene outside the place she would no longer be able to call home had made her vulnerable. Add to that all of Val's talk about how she shouldn't be so judgmental, how she should try to see the preppy hot male counselors with an unprejudiced eye, and you can understand how Carly might have briefly fallen into a mildly delusional state of infatuation with Stony Hollow's head sailing instructor.

When Cameron greeted them on the platform at the train station and started working his charm—taking their bags, teasing Jess out of her funk, asking Isabelle about her work as a college-placement counselor (and working in the fact that he went to Columbia)—she let herself be charmed.

Carly had her first five days at Stony Hollow free. They didn't need her in the kitchen yet since only the counselors were there for orientation. During those five days, Cameron seemed to pop up a lot. He gave her and Jess a tour of the camp, took them out on the lake a couple times, regaling them with stories about crewing boats in exotic places, and his own days as a Stony Hollow camper. He listened intently—or appeared to listen intently—to Jess's detailed summary of "Return to the Castle." Jess basked in Cameron's attentions. Sincere or not, cheering up Jess earned him bonus points in Carly's eyes.

Every night Carly would call and report to Val, whose "thing" (as she insisted on calling it) with Jake Alden, now interning at his father's investment bank, was progressing quickly. Val thought Cameron's actions indicated interest. And Jake thought so, too.

"You're telling Jake? Don't tell Jake."

"Why? He's not going to tell anyone."

"How do you know?"

"Because he's not like that. He doesn't gossip."

"But it's still embarrassing. Please?"

"Okay."

"Good. Can you go outside now?"

Every night Carly would ask Val to take her phone outside the restaurant so she could fill up on city noise. Isabelle always seemed to be in the camp office, and after Jess fell asleep, Carly found the sounds—and sometimes the silence—of the woods unnerving. With every twig snap and leaf crackle, she'd find herself thinking about the state prison she'd glimpsed out the train window on their way up, or about the rabid raccoon Cameron told her had terrorized the camp one summer, not too long ago. . . . If she could hear the swish of traffic, or a few bars of horn honking, or maybe the sound of a basketball hitting the pavement on the court next door to SJNY, then she'd be okay.

Carly had always considered herself an equal-opportunity-type person. She thought she was immune to the petty snobbery of places like Bellwin, where, if someone worked as a dishwasher, say, in the smelly, steamy kitchen of summer camp, you would dismiss them as being beneath you, unworthy of your attention.

But when she first met Brian, she did just that. Even though she was working in the same smelly, steamy kitchen, it simply didn't occur to her to think of the skinny townie dishwasher as a romantic prospect.

Never mind the pretty eyes. Or the sexy slouch.

The fact is, she hardly even noticed these attributes of Brian's when she met him on her first full day of actual work, the day Stony Hollow's two hundred campers arrived.

Even though most of the Stony Hollow food came frozen, canned, or dehydrated, Kevin the Cook dressed in a full chef's getup: checked pants, white, double-breasted jacket, and two-foot-high toque. He claimed to have graduated from the CIA, the Culinary Institute of America, which was nearby, but Carly had her doubts.

Kevin made no effort to hide his annoyance at being forced to employ Carly.

"You got any experience? Kitchenwise?"

"Not in the kitchen, but I have worked in a restaurant in Manhattan. SJNY?"

Carly wasn't sure if his grunt meant he had or hadn't heard of SJNY, but she decided not to press it.

She stood next to Kevin while he introduced her to the rest of the staff. "That's Louise, Rachel, and Sarah," he said, pointing to the three middle-aged women at the stove. "Ladies, this is Carly, Boss Lady's daughter." They looked up from their bubbling vats, waved plastic-gloved waves, and smiled.

"Do you think maybe you could not call me that?"

"It's your name, isn't it, Carly?"

He was smiling, daring Carly to challenge him. "Yes. Carly is my name. I meant the 'Boss Lady's Daughter' part."

"Oh. Okay. Hey, boys."

The three young dishwasher guys at the back of the kitchen kept right on talking to each other, oblivious. They were arguing. Something about a band. Whether the studio or live version of some song was better.

Kevin cupped his hands around his mouth and yelled louder. "Yo. Dudes."

They stopped arguing and looked at Kevin, who pointed

at and named each of them—Brian, Liam, Avery. Three variations on the same face: dark blue eyes beneath thick dark brows under thick black hair.

"Boys, meet the newest member of our humble kitchen staff. Carly. She's the daughter of Interim Director Isabelle . . . What's your last name, darlin'?"

"Mine's Finnegan. My mother's is Greene. But do you have to—"

"Interim Director Isabelle Greene."

The dishwashers greeted her with nods, chin lifts, and halfhearted *hey*s and went right back to their debate.

It was an exhausting first day. A lot went into feeding two hundred campers, and despite her alleged lack of experience, Kevin put a lot on Carly's shoulders. She peeled twenty pounds of carrots; calculated, measured, and mixed the proper amount of water with dehydrated brown gravy mix to produce enough for two hundred slices of meat loaf; and scooped globby, gelatinous chocolate pudding out of institutional-sized cans and into serving bowls. She'd never worked that hard for that long in her life, and when she'd plopped the last glob of pudding into its bowl, all she wanted was to get out of her sweaty work clothes, into a long hot shower, and down to the beach.

She knew what she was supposed to do with the cans. She knew she was supposed to rinse them, remove the labels and bottoms, and flatten them, then put them in the bright yellow recycling bin under the hand-lettered poster next to the garbage at the back of the kitchen:

Stony Hollow So Cares About Our Planet!!!

Normally she'd have been all over the recycling. She didn't need to be convinced with cheery posters or threatened with shame. She'd walked through enough of New York's junkyards with Nick to know a thing or two about waste. Seeing those vast mountains of everything from wrecked cars and broken refrigerators to Coke cans and beer bottles had done more to convince her than any public service announcement ever could.

But at that moment, she just didn't care. She just wanted out.

She made her way to the back of the kitchen, barely noticing Brian, who was scraping away at a baking pan crusted with mac and cheese. He didn't seem to notice her, either. He didn't look up as she threw the two empty pudding cans in the big plastic garbage bin and tossed the long-handled metal spoon in the pan of soapy water next to him. But then, as she was walking away, she heard the scraping stop and someone say, "Yo."

He didn't yell, but something about the way he said it—firmly, authoritatively—made Carly freeze. She turned around and found herself looking straight into Brian's eyes.

Blue and heavy-lidded, with lashes so thick and black you might wonder, on first seeing them, if cosmetics could be involved. Maybe dye? Of course, once you knew him, the idea of Brian Quinn standing in front of a mirror with a mascara wand in his hand or sitting in a chair at the salon was laughable.

"What do you think you're doing?"

"Just . . . cleaning up. Getting ready to leave."

"Those cans," he said, pointing his spatula at the pudding cans sitting on top of the garbage, "go in recycling."

"Oh." She smiled.

He glared.

"I'm totally with you on that, but I'm so tired. I'm dying to get in the shower."

He glared harder.

"Okay, okay. Relax." She walked back to the garbage and picked out the pudding cans, both now smeared with something slimy and yellow. She looked over her shoulder as she headed toward a sink on the other side of the kitchen.

He was watching her, smiling now, and it seemed like he had a whole different face. A not-scary, kind-of-even-maybe-nice face. For a townie dishwasher. He opened his mouth, like he was going to say something more to her, but stopped abruptly. Then he lifted one of his ear buds and cocked his head to listen, all the while keeping his eyes on Carly.

"Solo's still too long," he shouted over his shoulder.

"Dude, you say that about all my solos," came the response from the back of the room, where the other two townie dishwasher dudes—Brian's brother, Avery, and their cousin, Liam—were struggling to keep up with the campers' trays that had started rolling in on the conveyor belt and piling up against the back wall.

"Yeah, well, that's 'cause all your solos are too long."

The trays started coming faster. A lot faster. Plates of half-eaten meat loaf, congealed gravy, and lumpy mashed potatoes teetered on top of each other. Already a few plastic cups had fallen off and bounced along the tile floor at their feet. It was only a matter of time before everything came crashing down.

Avery stopped talking as he struggled to keep up, scraping the plates one by one into a garbage barrel next to him. Liam just stood there looking at the mess like he was afraid to move.

"Hit the button!" Brian didn't say "moron," but he didn't have to. The tone said it all.

Liam looked at Brian. "What button?"

"Up there! On the wall." While Liam looked around clueless, Brian ran over, elbowed Avery out of the way, jumped up, and slapped the bright red button marked

EMERGENCY SHUTOFF on the wall. The conveyor belt stopped. Plates and silverware continued to clatter for a few seconds. A lone plastic cup fell to the floor and rattled its way across the kitchen. Then all was still.

"Two words, brother," Avery said, like nothing had happened. "Jimi. And Hendrix."

"Three words, brother," Brian responded, counting the words off on one hand while stacking plates with the other. "In. Your. Dreams. But keep practicing. You never know."

No one seemed to be paying attention to Carly anymore, so she started toward the back door, thinking about that shower.

"Ah—ah—come back here, Earth Destroyer. I'm not letting you off that easy."

So she did as she was told. She rinsed and flattened the cans, put them into the proper receptacle, and scurried away dreaming dreamy dreams of a summer romance with Cameron Foster.

"Hey, Carly." Cameron smelled faintly of shaving cream, and the ends of his hair tickled Carly's neck. He pressed the wet, cold beer bottle against the exposed skin of her upper arm. "Glad you could make it. Do you know everyone?" He turned her toward the big rock at the edge of the water, where most of the counselors were spread out, talking in pairs and small groups. "Come on." Cameron started walking toward a big rock at the edge of the water, where two girls she recognized as tennis instructors were sprawled out. "Anna, Lucy, have you met Carly?"

Without so much as raising their heads, they looked Carly up and down. One said, "Hey." The other half-raised a hand, in something resembling a wave, like she wasn't sure Carly was worth the trouble.

"Carly's Isabelle's daughter."

That got their attention. They both sat up, wide-eyed, nervously looking at their beer bottles.

"Oh, don't worry. She's cool." Cameron winked. "Right, Carly? You're not going to rat us out for drinking on camp grounds or anything, are you?" He reached into the side pocket of his cargo shorts and pulled out a silver flask. He screwed off the top and offered it to her.

She took the flask and lifted it toward her mouth. The fumes stung her nose. "Don't worry," she said, and to show them just how much they could trust her, she guzzled. She got three full swallows down before her throat felt like it was closing itself. She handed the flask back to Cameron, gasped out "Thanks," and sat down.

The rock was still warm from the sun. She closed her eyes and took in a long, slow breath of the night air. Mixed in with smell of wood smoke was the dank and fishy smell that seemed to permeate Stony Hollow. She thought she was going to be sick, but then a pine-scented breeze came off the lake, and she managed to calm her churning stomach. She was pleasantly buzzed, enjoying the company of the Stony Hollow counselors and the illusion of Cameron Foster's interest.

As she sat there, listening to Cameron's tales of adventure crewing a boat that sailed from Maine to Puerto Rico the summer before, she imagined what it would be like to be with Cameron. On a night like this, on the open sea, just the two of them. When Cameron offered the flask a second time, Carly took two even bigger swigs, pausing to breathe in between. And when someone offered her a bottle of something bright red and very sweet, she gladly accepted and drank it down like it was soda.

Which it wasn't.

As long as she was lying against the warm rock, it didn't matter that she felt like she was on a boat. It was actually kind of nice, closing her eyes and imagining herself on the sea with Cameron Foster as her only companion.

But the second her feet hit the ground, that pleasant sensation of being gently rocked on the water turned into the feeling of being tossed around in a major storm. One step and she knew she was in trouble. She was on her way down to the ground when Cameron and Ben Marcus, one of the tennis guys, caught her, one on each side.

"Whoa."

The two of them steered, dragged, and carried her back to the cabin she shared with her mother. Luckily for Carly, her mother was spending most of her time in her office, combing apartment listings online or talking on the phone with her sister Nancy, reviewing the last days of her and Nick.

As Carly wobbled along, she told them all about how she wasn't supposed to be at Stony Hollow but in Turkey, with her famous—in archaeological circles—father who revolutionized the study of the ancient Greek safety pin.

They didn't seem to appreciate the significance.

And then she barfed. On Cameron Foster's feet. The neon pink puke glowed against the dark brown of his Top-Siders.

"I'm sorry. I'm sorry. I'm so, so sorry."

"It's cool. It's cool." The look of disgust on his face and the way he practically shoved her onto her bed said it wasn't.

10

SHE WOKE up dizzy and nauseous and humiliated, wishing she'd chosen to spend her summer among the juvenile delinquents and Amish of Ohio. She dragged herself to the kitchen and tried not to gag when she walked into a cloud of sausage-flavored steam.

The hair-netted ladies were chirping away over their bubbling vats; the dishwasher guys were quiet, each plugged into his own iPod.

Kevin gave her a list of stomach-turning tasks she needed to finish by the midafternoon break. It started with scrambling the liquid-egg equivalent of two hundred eggs and ended with dishing out that night's dessert of artificially flavored banana pudding. In between, she was supposed to spread two hundred previously frozen chicken legs out on four giant baking dishes.

The chicken legs brought her seriously close to vomiting for the second time in less than twelve hours. She hadn't so much as touched a cooked chicken leg in a couple of years. The raw ones, with their pink-gray flesh under all that saggy, yellow skin, were just too much. After laying the first fifty out in five rows of ten, she had to go outside for air.

When she came back in, all four baking dishes were lined with legs. The bags they'd been in were nowhere to be seen, and the stainless-steel counter had been cleaned to Kevin's exacting standards.

Carly looked around the kitchen, trying to figure out who had come to her rescue. The dishwasher guys were busy with the pots and pans the hairnetted cooks kept delivering to them. The hairnetted cooks were way too busy trying to keep up with the lunch line. Kevin was nowhere to be seen.

She moved on to the pudding. That was a lot easier because she didn't have to have any actual contact with the stuff. As long as she could avoid breathing in through her nose and thereby avoid the too-sweet smell of artificial banana flavoring, she'd be okay.

While she was scooping the pudding, she caught sight of Cameron in the dining room through the conveyor-belt window. He was laughing it up with the beautiful Julia McMillan, head girls' counselor.

"Ah, the other half." She hadn't heard him come up behind her. But there was Brian, standing to her left, looking out at Cameron and Julia.

"See how they live," said Avery, standing on Carly's other side.

"What?" she scooped faster and tried to act like she didn't know what they were talking about.

"The beautiful people. They're so . . ."

"Bee-oo-ti-ful," said Avery, in falsetto, holding his arms out to the side like some maniacal ballerina. He clasped his hands together, pressed them to his cheek, and batted his eyelashes at Brian. "Oh, Sailor Boy, what *strong tanned arms* you have."

Brian stuck his chest out and held his arms stiffly at his sides. His rendition of Cameron's smirk was dead-on. He deepened his voice to a mock manly man's. "Yeah, well. Comes with the territory, honey. Did you know I've won several national sailing competitions, including the Single-Handed Championship? And, by the way, there's no 'team' in 'Single-Handed.'"

Carly laughed. This tidbit of Cameron Foster's biography—along with the news that he'd be entering Columbia in the fall—was prominently featured on the Stony Hollow Web site below a picture of him turning about or lowering the boom or whatever it is that Single-Handed Sailing Champions single-handedly do.

Twenty-four hours before, she'd been swooning over the details of his résumé while using the wireless connection in her mother's office. Now, with Brian reciting it, it all sounded silly.

"Really?" Avery widened his eyes and put a hand on each cheek. "That's such a coincidence! Did you know that I hold the scoring record in field hockey for the National Independent Schools Athletic Association and will be attending a prestigious liberal arts college in New England in the fall?"

These facts could also be found on the camp Web site, under a close-up of Julia's beautiful, lightly freckled face.

Maybe these townie guys weren't so bad. Maybe working in the kitchen would turn out to be fun.

Avery disappeared, and Brian asked how she was feeling.

"Fine," she said, as the blood rose to her cheeks.

"Really? Working with food isn't exactly the best cure for a hangover."

"Tell me about it." Wait. How did he—? "How did you know?"

"Saw you."

"You saw me?"

"Actually heard you first. Me and my brother were on our way home, and we heard this girl kind of yelling, and we were worried. So we followed the sound, and then we saw you and Sailor Boy and Tennis Guy. Man, you're a loud drunk."

Usually when Carly was about to cry, her body gave her enough advance notice to prepare. Her nose tingled and the back of her throat tightened and her ears would get really, really hot. But this time, there was no warning.

"Hey," Brian said, but she ignored him. "Hey." He put

a hand on her shoulder. She tried to pull away, but he held firm. "Hey."

She turned around, steeling herself for a knowing look, a snarky smirk. But what she saw was a smile, and those eyes, looking right into hers, not mocking but concerned.

"I didn't mean to—"

The tears were way out of proportion to anything that had just happened. It was like she'd been saving everything up—her disappointment about Turkey, the shock of having to move out of her home of twelve years, of getting way too much information about her mother and Nick's now-dead relationship, the humiliation of the Pink Vomit Incident.

Carly was a sniveling mess, and she should have been embarrassed, but for some reason she wasn't. And Brian, who should have been disgusted by the effluvia flowing from her orifices, didn't seem to be, judging by what he did next.

He said, "I know a really good hangover cure." Then he took the serving spoon out of her hand and put it in Avery's. "Finish this up, okay? This girl needs a trip to the Rock. Meet us there."

He took Carly by her hand and gently but firmly pulled her through the kitchen. As they passed through the back door, he shouted one more order over his shoulder. "Someone grab my board shorts." He pulled her past the

Dumpsters, past the old broken-down tables and obsolete kitchen equipment rusting under the brown tarp, onto a path through the woods.

She followed him into the woods even though there was nothing to keep her from leaving. She never, for one second, felt like she was in danger.

Except maybe of losing her job, which just moments before she'd been thinking of quitting, but suddenly wanted desperately to keep.

"What about Kevin?"

"What about him?"

"Isn't he going to be pissed that we left early?"

"Kevin? Nah. He doesn't care who gets what done, as long as it gets done. Those guys'll make sure everything's cool before they leave."

"Where are we were going?"

"You'll see."

They followed a complicated route along intersecting paths until they hit a set of old train tracks, which they followed to a dirt road, which they followed to another path.

After a while the path disappeared, and they were walking on a bed of fallen pine needles so thick that it absorbed the sound of their footsteps. Soon the dark green of the pines opened up onto a thin strip of beach.

Two huge rocks rose out of the ground and extended far into the lake. On one of the rocks, three or four teenage girls in neon bikinis lay out on beach towels. Five or six guys in trunks stood at the outermost edge of the other rock, taking turns jumping and diving.

A little while after she and Brian stepped into the sunlight, Liam and Avery appeared, as if out of thin air. The pine needles must have absorbed the sounds of their footsteps, too. They'd both changed into board shorts; Avery tossed Brian his.

Together the three of them told Carly all about Baldwin Rock. Unofficial Townie Beach, accessible only through that complicated route of semisecret paths handed down through generations of locals.

"Once in a while," Avery said, "the Citiots hear about it and try to blend in with the locals."

"Citiots?"

Citiots, they explained, were a particular breed of rich city people.

"The ones who think that just because they spend a half a mill on an old termite-infested farmhouse . . ." Avery offered.

"Strip it down to the studs and then spend *another* million," Liam added.

"Or two or three," said Brian. "I heard those people who bought the old Flynn place spent *three*."

Avery shook his head. "No way. Three? On what?"

"For starters, they went and bought *two* more houses up in Maine or New Hampshire or someplace like that, then wrecked 'em, just for the wood, and the sinks and light fixtures."

"Oh, man," Avery shook his head. "That's just wrong."

Brian nodded.

Carly knew those people. Not those exact people, but people like them. They lived in her building. What used to be her building. Went to Bellwin. One girl in the middle school had her bathroom featured in the *New York Times* the year before. Her parents spent a hundred thousand dollars to make it look like a tropical paradise, complete with a fake waterfall shower, steam room, and sauna.

"Okay, now," Brian said, pointing to the water as he started back into the woods. "That there is the world's best hangover cure. I recommend no further delay. I'll be right back."

"But I don't have my suit." It was a lame thing to say. Her cutoffs and tank top would do just fine. But no one heard her say it. Brian had disappeared, and Liam and Avery sprinted into the water.

She'd gone swimming at the camp beach with Jess a couple times during orientation week and found the water frigid and silty. But from here the lake looked clear. It smelled sweet, too. There was no trace of the dank fishiness that hung in the air on the other side. If she couldn't see the Stony Hollow dock with the line of kids waiting their turn on the slide directly across, she would have thought it was a different body of water.

She took a running start and dove in.

Floating on her back in the cool water, face to the sun, she felt the hangover drain away. She felt like she'd entered a new world. A right-side-up world where buying two extra houses so you could renovate a third with the right wood and the right sinks was seen for the crazy excess that it was; a world where people like Cameron Foster and Julia McMillan weren't looked up to or envied or longed for but laughed at.

A world that contained a certain blue-eyed boy. A boy who knew about the Pink Vomit Incident and had already seen her cry but seemed to like her anyway.

This was the world she belonged in.

FOR THE next three days, Carly went to Baldwin Rock with the boys every afternoon. There was no invitation. No one said, *Carly, would you care to join us?* It was just somehow understood when Kevin dismissed them for the afternoon break that they were all going.

Brian didn't take Carly's hand on those afternoon trips to the lake, but he did walk by her side. And on those walks they had conversations. Not superficial small talk, but real back-and-forth asking and listening about each other's lives. By the end of those three days, Brian knew about Carly's love of archaeology and the canceled trip to Aphrodisias and having to move out of the loft. And Carly knew the broad outlines of Brian's life: that he'd lived in Brooklyn until his father died, then he and Avery and their mother had moved upstate to "Ernestine's," which is what everybody called their grandmother's house, even now that she'd been dead for a year. Ernestine's property bordered Stony Hollow, and her kids had worked there when they were growing up. Liam, their cousin, lived down the road, and the three of them had been playing music together in the shed behind Ernestine's on instruments that had belonged to their fathers since before they could remember. Now they were a band called Quinn.

"That's it, Quinn? Just Quinn?" she asked.

"Yup. Quinn. No *s*, no *The*, no *Boys*. Just Quinn."

The band name was Ernestine's idea. She'd been their biggest fan. She loved that her grandsons spent hours in that shed working on their music, especially after losing Brian's father, her first-born son. She paid for a new roof, heat, and insulation, and had it wired for electricity so they could use their amps and run their recording equipment out there. She was the only adult in the family who encouraged them to aim high, the only one who didn't freak out about their wanting to put college off to concentrate on music.

Before she died, Ernestine helped them negotiate The Plan: they could take one year after Liam and Avery graduated from high school to "make something happen" with the band. (Brian was a year older and had graduated the year before.) During that year, they would only have to work part-time day jobs to pay for band expenses like gas and upkeep for the van, recording equipment, and instrument care. They could live at Ernestine's for as long as they wanted to save money. Food would be paid for out of a small fund she was leaving them in her will. If there weren't "clear signs of progress"—in the form of regular paying gigs or movement toward a recording contract—after the year was up, they would go to college or get serious, career-type jobs.

According to Brian, they were ahead of schedule. Liam and Avery had just graduated in June, and they already had a small local following from playing frat parties around SUNY New Paltz. They had gigs that summer at the all-ages club in town and the one frat house that stayed open for summer school, but mostly they were working on their demo. In the fall they were moving back to Brooklyn to try to break into the New York scene. A booking agent had promised to get them gigs in the city if the demo came out well. Brian's mother had rented their Brooklyn house out but kept the basement apartment open for her and the boys to use for visits to the city.

Despite all the getting-to-know-you talk, Carly still wasn't sure what, if anything, was going on between her and Brian until the night he invited her back to Ernestine's.

"It might be boring, listening to us record. But hey, if you like archaeology, the shed's got stuff going back to before Ernestine's was Ernestine's. You could poke around there if you get bored."

"Okay." Carly didn't think she was going to get bored, but she liked that Brian was thinking about what might make her happy. It had been a while since anyone had done that.

Later that evening she was sitting in a dusty old arm-chair crammed between an amp and a cobwebbed window in the shed behind Ernestine's. Brian and Avery and Liam were busy plugging guitars into amps, amps into extension cords, extension cords into extension cords. Testing connections, running scales.

As much as she liked Brian by then, she wasn't expecting much. She figured they were just another trio of wannabe rock-star boys, one of thousands of bands messing around in garages, basements, and sheds all over the country.

Then she heard that first song and she knew they were good.

Really good.

They made her think if Nick, who, whenever he talked about music would go on about "clean and tight rock 'n' roll you got with just a guitar, bass, and drums" like his favorites, The Ramones. Not that their music was anything like the Ramones'. Quinn's was lighter, more playful and melodic. But raw, somehow, too.

Avery had the chops and the looks and the stage presence of a sexy front man. He sang into the microphone like it was a lover, even when there was no one but his brother and cousin and this girl who scooped pudding in a camp kitchen there to see him.

Liam wailed on drums.

But Brian was the one to watch. The only one Carly

wanted to watch. Head down, eyes closed, fingers dancing over the long neck of his bass, giving the music its pulse.

The songs were his, too. He wrote all the originals. Some of them were funny/sweet tributes to everyday people, like "Mailman":

You got to be there
Six days a week

And "Lunch Lady":

Ladles her love
On ev-er-y-one.

Others, like "Everybody Does It," which was about a girl who gets caught shoplifting a shirt she thinks will make her beautiful, told whole stories. In addition to these originals, they played an eclectic mix of covers from the seventies and eighties. Everything from Bruce Springsteen to Queen to R.E.M. to Talking Heads, Blondie, the Clash, and assorted disco favorites in quirky arrangements. They'd slow fast songs down, speed the slow ones up, add a reggae beat here, a rap riff there, and three-part harmonies where you'd never expect to find them.

After practice Brian took Carly on a tour. Ernestine's had lots of small, weirdly shaped rooms, some with numbers on the doors because, he explained, it had originally been a boardinghouse for workers building the aqueduct, the huge underground tunnel system that carries water from the mountains to the city.

Brian's room was number nine. The only one up on the third floor. It was small, with sloped walls. Carly wasn't a neat freak, and she wouldn't have held it against him if it had been a mess, but she was relieved to see that the futon on the floor was made, with two pillows side-by-side. No stray underwear to avert her eyes from. No socks in strange places.

"You gotta see my view." He walked to the window, gesturing for her to follow. He slid the screen up, sat on the windowsill, swung his legs around and over it, and scrambled out onto the roof. He sat down and patted the spot next to him. "Come on out."

"Uh—" Carly sat on the sill with her feet firmly on the floor, and looked down three stories to the weathered picnic table below. "That's okay."

It was the end of dusk. The trees made a thick, leafy silhouette against the orange-pink sky.

"It's perfectly safe. I wouldn't let you if it wasn't."

"I believe you." She did. The roof's slant wasn't steep. It looked like it would actually be hard to fall off. But she couldn't talk her heart out of pounding, or her head out of imagining herself splayed out on the table below. She would have liked nothing more than to be sitting on the spot where his hand was. But "I just can't," she said. "At least not right now."

He scooted back toward the window, and she thought he was going to try to talk her into it, but he didn't. Instead he leaned against the window frame and pointed.

"See the clearing over there?"

She followed his pointing hand to the woods across the road.

"Not really. All I see are trees."

"Ah. That's 'cause you're looking through city eyes."

"City eyes?"

"Yeah. I had city eyes before we moved up here full-time. Used to all be one big green blur."

"That's pretty much what I'm seeing. A big green blur."

"Seeing in the woods is like seeing in the dark. Takes a while. But once your eyes get adjusted, you see so much more. Like I bet right now you can't see those deer across the road."

She looked where he was pointing but still saw nothing but trees. She shook her head.

"Just past that first row of trees, see? How the green blur opens up a bit?"

"Nope. Still a blur."

It was true. It wasn't a ploy to get Brian to move closer. But he did move closer. Close enough that he could put his hand on the underside of her cheek and direct her gaze. His fingertips were rough. Dried out from washing dishes and calloused from the strings of his bass. Carly liked the feeling of his scratchy skin on hers.

"See?"

"Yeah." Now she saw the break in the trees. It ran parallel to the road and disappeared over a small hill.

"That's the footpath that runs over the aqueduct. Now look down, just to the right of that—" Gently he pulled her face downward, and she saw something moving under the trees. She squinted and three small deer came into focus. They were feeding on the grass and brush.

"I see them!"

It was getting darker. Fireflies sparkled among the trees.

"Let's go over there."

Ernestine's living room had an incredibly low ceiling. Brian's hair brushed against it as they made their way toward the kitchen, where his mother stood at the sink, her long red hair clipped in a haphazard twist. Between the sound of running water and the radio blaring a baseball game, she didn't hear them until Brian half-yelled, "Hey, Ma. What's the score?"

Without turning around, she said, "It's 4–2 Chicago. A-Rod dropped a pop fly that should have been a double play."

Brian scowled, shook his head. "That guy better start earning his salary."

She turned around, a huge head of dark green and purple lettuce in her hand. She was pretty. Younger than Carly's mother. Or maybe just better rested. Freckly and blue-eyed. Brian and Avery must get the dark from their father's side.

"Tell me about it."

She held the lettuce over the sink and shook out the water before placing it next to two smaller heads on a blue-checked kitchen towel spread on the counter. On the other side of the sink there was a handbasket full of tomatoes, cucumbers, and various leafy, stalky things. Next to that, a colander of dark red cherries. She reached over and turned the game down to where the crowd's roar sounded like static.

"So?" She smiled at Carly. It was the same broad smile as her sons', but with some sadness visible in her eyes. "You going to introduce us? Or do I have to do it myself?"

"Oh, sorry. Ma, this is Carly. Carly, this is my ma, Sheryl Quinn."

"Hey, Carly," she said, offering her cool, slightly damp hand.

"Hi, Sheryl."

"Carly works at the camp with us." He stepped over to the counter and grabbed a handful of cherries. "Wow," he said, tipping his head toward the basket of vegetables. "Did you pick all this?"

"Yup," Sheryl said, smiling. "I think we finally foiled the rabbits."

"*We* did, huh?"

"Yup. Thanks to the brilliant fence building of my sons, of course." Sheryl reached a hand up to Brian's shoulder. Brian put an arm around his mother's waist and squeezed her close.

Carly found herself blushing at this display of mother-son affection, and she looked down so they could have their private moment. But when she looked up, Sheryl and Brian were leaning back against the counter together, each still with an arm around the other. Each smiling at her.

"So, Carly, you from around here?"

Carly shook her head. "The city."

Brian reached out and dangled a cherry in front of Carly's mouth by its stem. She was too embarrassed to bite standing there talking to his mother and instead took it with her hand.

"What part?"

Carly put the cherry in her mouth, letting the cool, smooth skin rest on her tongue for a second before biting. It was juicier and sweeter than any she'd had all summer. Possibly her whole life.

"We're kind of between parts right now." She took the

pit from her mouth and looked around for somewhere to put it. Seeing none, she slipped it into the little pocket-inside-the-pocket at the front of her cutoffs. "We used to live downtown, on the West Side."

Sheryl nodded and looked down at her bare feet. Her toenails were painted a deep, purply red, and she wore a silver toe ring on her right foot.

"So what brings you to Snotty Hollow?"

Carly gave her the short version, making it sound like her mother was there to do her friends a favor, without mentioning the part about their needing the money, or her mother and Nick breaking up.

Sheryl and Brian explained that "Snotty Hollow" was a Quinn family joke. Something Ernestine came up with back when her kids worked summer jobs there.

"She grew up in Ireland, where no one went to sleep-away camp," Brian said.

"She couldn't believe parents would send their kids away for four or eight weeks at a time and pay outrageous money for them to have the privilege of running around in the woods and swimming in the lake," said Sheryl. "Her kids did that for free every day."

"Yeah, well, you're forgetting about archery," Carly offered. "You want your kid to get somewhere in this world, she's gotta know her bows from her arrows, and for that, you gotta cough up the cash."

Brian and Sheryl both laughed. Sheryl tilted her head

toward Carly and said to her son, "Ernestine would like this one."

He smiled and looked at Carly. "Yeah. Ernestine would've liked Carly."

Sheryl turned the radio back up. The crowd was roaring. "Whoa. What'd I miss?"

"And strrrrrike three brings us to the bottom of the eighth here in Chicago. The score is 5–4 New York."

"See ya, Ma." Brian started toward the door at the back of the kitchen.

"Wait," Sheryl said, reaching for the colander. "You guys take these." She pulled a few paper towels off a roll on the counter, dumped the cherries into it, and handed the bundle to Carly.

There was nothing remarkable about the footpath, no way to tell from above that just a few hundred feet below was a tunnel through which the New York City water supply flowed on its way downstate from the Catskill Mountains.

"Really?" Carly pointed to the path, well worn with footprints and bicycle-tire treads. "Right here?"

"Yup," Brian said. "Pretty cool, huh? I used to stand out here when I was little and imagine I could feel the water swishing past on its way to Brooklyn. And then when I was back there, sometimes, when I was drinking from the water fountain at school, or taking a shower, or washing my dad's car, I'd picture this exact spot and wonder what was happening here at that moment. What birds were here, hunting what bugs. If the rabbits were out, or the deer."

He stared at the ground, as if he could see the water moving below it, the trace of a smile on his face.

"How did he die?"

Brian didn't look up. "World Trade Center."

Carly knew Brian's father had been a fireman and that he'd died when the boys were little. But she'd somehow gotten the impression that he'd been sick.

She couldn't think of anything to say except "I'm sorry."

Brian put his hands in his pockets. "Yeah."

"That must've been—must be—"

"It's okay. I mean—it's not okay—what happened. Obviously. I mean, it's okay, you don't have to try to find the right thing to say. There is no right thing to say."

Carly nodded, relieved.

They walked along the path awhile longer, neither saying anything. Fireflies blinked, crickets chirped while the sky went from a blue-pink glow to dark blue to just dark.

Carly thought back to that day. How school just stopped when the news came. She was in Ms. Wilson's language arts class discussing *Little Women*. The question was why Laurie (the boy next door) would want to marry Amy after being in love with Jo, and people were getting upset. Most of the girls in the class identified with Jo, but there was a faction, led by Piper Peterson, who thought Jo was "a little over-the-top and probably a lesbian" and claimed they'd rather be Amy any day.

In the middle of the debate Ms. Goldhaber, the head of the middle school, knocked on the door and asked to speak with Ms. Wilson out in the hall. After a few minutes Ms. Wilson came back ashen faced and told the girls in a trembling voice to gather their things and head for the cafeteria. No one knew what was happening, but somehow they all knew it was serious, and no one uttered a word as they made their way down the echoing hallway.

Carly looked at Brian, who kept his eyes on the path beneath them. "I can't imagine—"

"I'll tell you about it sometime."

"Okay."

"But not now." Brian looked up, reached for her hand, and pulled her to the side of the path next to a huge tree.

"Okay."

He leaned back against the tree and with his other reached around and loosened the clip holding her hair.

With her other hand she tried to contain the mass of curls that spilled out. The summer heat and kitchen humidity were making them more unruly than ever.

"Hey. Don't do that. I love your hair."

"You do?"

"Yeah. I do." He was holding both her hands, and he

didn't let go as he circled her waist with his arms. "Your hair was the first thing I noticed about you."

They were nose to nose, eye to eye. His breath smelled of cherries.

She tried to say "It was?" but by then her lips were otherwise engaged.

When they came up for air Brian said, "That was nice."

To which Carly could say only "Mmmm" because as he said it, he reached under her shirt and with the calloused tips of his fingers, lightly stroked his way from her lower back, around the sides of her waist and across her belly, leaving her not only speechless but barely able to stand.

At the point where Carly was considering saving herself the trouble of falling and instead throwing herself to the ground and taking him with her, he pulled away and said, "We better get you back."

Why? she wanted to ask but didn't. As much as she didn't want to stop, she liked that stopping was his idea.

When they got back to the cabin, her mother's bedside light was still on, but through the gauzy curtains they could see that she was out, mouth open, eyes closed behind her funky purple reading glasses, book lying open against her chest. So they sat on the steps and kissed again, more lightly this time, with only lips touching. Then they said good night.

Isabelle didn't wake up when Carly tiptoed across the

creaky floorboards of the cabin. She barely stirred when Carly slipped her reading glasses off and put her book, *When Things Fall Apart: Heart Advice for Difficult Times*, on her nightstand.

That night, for the first time since she'd left the city, Carly didn't freak out every time a twig snapped or a leaf crackled. She didn't feel the need to call Val for the reassuring sounds of the city. She'd call Val, of course. What had happened with Brian was huge news. But she'd wait till the morning.

Now all she wanted to do was lie on her bed replaying everything, in super slo-mo. From the first to the last kiss and everything in between. When she closed her eyes she could still feel the calloused tips of Brian's fingers traveling across her torso. She could still smell the lake water and lemony dish soap on his skin.

She could still taste the cherries.

It wasn't like this with Harris Gibson, that sort-of boyfriend she'd had for a couple of months at the end of her sophomore year.

They'd met in a psychology class she took at Edward G. Champion when they were assigned to do a research project together on Jean Piaget's theories of cognitive development. One afternoon when they were working at Harris's apartment they just started kissing. Carly couldn't say for sure whose idea it was. One minute they were debating how many slides they should have in their Power-Point presentation, and the next they were rolling around on his couch.

Her relationship with Harris was kind of a research project in itself, the object of which was to figure out how far you could go with someone you liked well enough but didn't spend much (if any) time thinking about when you weren't together.

The answer, she learned, was pretty far once you got started.

After those first kisses at his apartment, they'd always end up messing around whenever they got together to work on their presentation. And then even after the presentation was over, they kept getting together, always with the stated purpose of studying. But the studying never lasted very long. They'd always somehow start kissing and then move on to touching and rubbing and all that.

Except not *that*.

But if Harris Gibson hadn't left the city for computer-programming camp at Yale that summer, it might have eventually come to that.

For about a week after he left, they kept up a half-hearted electronic flirtation. They even toyed with the idea of Carly getting on a train to New Haven and taking advantage of the away-from-home-and-living-in-a-dorm situation. When he blew her off in a text, telling her he'd met someone else, she didn't feel so much as a twinge of hurt or regret or damaged pride. More like relief.

Now Harris's meeting MIT-bound Stephanie at Yale seemed like one more link in the carefully arranged, everything-happens-for-a-reason chain of events leading her to Brian.

Brian would be her first. And it would be totally right.

She was ready.

Very ready.

And so glad Harris Gibson went to Yale.

Val didn't get it.

"How can you possibly know that, after one night of making out?"

And Carly didn't get Val.

"I just do, that's all. I can't explain it. I've never felt this way before. *Never.* I want it to be him." When she'd woken up that morning, the first thing she'd done was text Val about Brian. About how amazing it had been to kiss him under the stars. How she could see herself going all the way with him. Now it was midmorning. Val had just gotten up, and Carly was out back, behind the kitchen, flattening the day's cans with her feet while they talked on the phone.

"The dishwasher-slash-rock-star is going to be your first? You've already made up your mind?"

"Jeez. Be a little judgmental, why don't you? I can't believe I'm hearing this from you. You haven't even met him, but you think you know all about him because of his job."

"Carly. Let's review what I do know—from you: One, he's nineteen, almost twenty, and still living with his mother in his grandmother's house."

"*You* live with your grandmother!"

"That's different. I'm still in high school; where am I supposed to live?"

"Yeah. Okay. But they're living there to save money. They have a plan."

"Uh-huh. Two, he's not going to college."

"Yet. He's not going to college *yet*. He's going to see what happens with the music."

"Do you know how many people say they're postponing college and then never go?"

"No. Do you?"

"No. But you should ask your mother. I'm sure it's a lot."

"Great. Yeah. I'll ask my mom. She's such a font of romantic wisdom."

"I didn't say that. But the woman does know a thing or two about going to college."

"Did she talk to you? Is this, like, some plot the two of you hatched?"

"Are you serious?"

"I don't know, maybe. I've never heard you talk like this before."

"Like what?"

"Like judging people by what they do for a living. How much money they have. I guess maybe you are a real Bellwin girl after all."

"Oh, right. That is not what I'm doing, Carly. It's not about money or what people do for a living. I just think maybe . . . possibly . . . you're rushing things here. A few days ago it was all about the sailing guy—what was his name?"

"Cameron."

"Yeah. And now, in the space of, like, forty-eight hours, you're throwing yourself at someone else."

"I am not throwing myself at him!" Though she had, in the passion of the moment, briefly contemplated throwing herself down on the ground the night before. Normally Carly would have shared that bit of information with Val, and they would have laughed about it. But something was changing. She kept it to herself.

"No? That's what it sounds like."

"And you don't know him."

"It's true. I don't know him. And I don't think you know him well enough to know if it's right. *Yet*. You can't know *yet*. Can you grant me that?"

"Okay. I'll grant you that. I can't know yet." But she knew. She had no doubt. She just wasn't going to fight about it with Val.

12

FROM THEN on, Carly and Brian spent almost all their time together. Instead of lingering until the last possible moment after her alarm went off, she'd jump out of bed at dawn, eager to see him. She would breeze through whatever grunt work Kevin assigned her, knowing that when it was over, she'd get to be with Brian.

They went to Baldwin Rock every afternoon during their break, or back to Ernestine's to play cards or Monopoly or watch a movie when it rained.

Evenings, after she was done dishing out dessert, she would take a shower while the guys finished washing the dishes and stacking them in the dining hall for the next day's breakfast. Then they would meet behind the kitchen and head over to Ernestine's. Carly didn't mind hanging out while they practiced or put down tracks for their demo. Sometimes she'd sit in the cobwebby corner listening or reading.

Sometimes she'd poke around in the shed, playing archaeologist.

It was a lot like an archaeological site back there, with layers from different eras. Apparently Ernestine never threw anything away. She just piled it all up in the shed. Five decades of Quinn family stuff, the most recent on top: plastic pots from Stone Ridge Nurseries, circa 2003; a broken answering machine from the 1990s; a big, heavy computer monitor; tennis rackets, one of them made of wood and warped from years in the shed. There were dust-covered sleds and ice skates that had belonged to Brian's father and his siblings; Ernestine's old 1950s sewing machine. There was even a box full of stuff that had been found over the years in the crawl spaces between the closets and up in the attic. Little bits and pieces from the boardinghouse days. Beer bottles buried in the yard, faded playing cards, scraps of newspaper. One funny-looking work boot stiff with age that Brian said he thought had belonged to one of the aqueduct workers.

Sometimes she hung out with Sheryl while she watered and puttered in her vegetable garden or listened to a Yankees game on the radio. Sheryl liked to tell stories about the days before her husband died.

After band practice, Brian and Carly would walk out on the aqueduct trail, stopping at the tree where they first kissed, making out while the dusky sky went dark.

Whenever things got hot, he would be the one to pull away, saying something like, "It's getting late. We better get you home." As if there were some shotgun-toting father whose curfew Carly dared not break, waiting at the window for her safe and chaste return.

"Good," said Val. "He's not pressuring you."

"Of course he isn't pressuring me. I told you, he's not like that."

"I know. I know. He's perfect." Despite her promise to keep an open mind, Val obviously still had her doubts and wasn't making much of an attempt to hide them. This was hard for Carly, who wanted to be able to share her happiness with her best friend.

"What about Jake?"

"What about him?"

"Is he pressuring you?"

"No. . . . He doesn't have to pressure me."

"You mean—?"

"Yup."

"When?"

"Couple nights ago."

"And when were you going to tell me?"

"I'm telling you now."

"Because I asked?"

"No. No. I was going to tell you. I just—I haven't told anyone else. Don't worry. I just wanted to keep it to myself for a little while."

"Oh."

- - -

Carly didn't want to keep things to herself. She wanted to share what was happening between her and Brian with her best friend. She knew that if Val could only meet Brian, she'd stop with all the judging and assumptions. If Val had a chance to see what Carly saw, know the guy Carly knew, then she couldn't help but be happy for her.

She tried to get Val to come up and see for herself one Saturday when the guys were supposed to play a party at a frat house.

"A frat party?"

"Brian says it'll be low-key because there aren't as many people around during the summer."

"Yeah, but a frat party?"

"It's not about the party, Val. It's so you can meet him, see them play. Come on. You can get one night off."

Val said she'd ask her mother and call back. Five minutes later she called to report that Angela allegedly nixed the idea because they were short-handed at SJNY. "Everybody's taking their vacation so she needs me."

Carly knew that things got like that in summer, when a lot of the full-time staff went back home. But it didn't sound like Val had tried very hard to convince her mother, either.

Isabelle didn't need much—any, really—convincing to let Carly go to the gig with Brian. She expressed some concern about how late things would go, but after getting Carly's assurance that she'd be home no later than one A.M. and that she wouldn't complain about getting up the next day for work, Isabelle relented.

It was almost too easy.

The night of the frat party, after finishing work and before it was time for the boys to pick her up, Carly brought her laptop down to the camp office, where there was wireless, to e-mail her father. He'd sent her a series of sonograms of the shrimp that was supposed to grow into another little sister, and judging by the exclamation points in his e-mail, he expected some measure of enthusiasm in response.

Isabelle was there, too, combing apartment listings and returning parents' phone calls.

Running Stony Hollow had turned out to be much harder than she'd imagined. Every day brought a new crisis. The homesick kid who wouldn't stop crying in bunk two, the head-lice invasion in bunk seven. It seemed like when she wasn't fixing a crisis, she was explaining it to parents.

"These people," she said, after hanging up from what sounded like a particularly exasperating conversation. "If I could afford to send my kids away, I wouldn't be spending every day worrying about them."

"Thanks, Mom," Carly said from behind her computer.

"Oh, *pffft*. You know what I mean. I'd worry. Of course I'd worry. But I wouldn't harass the people who were taking care of my kids. *Trying* to take care of my kids. I wouldn't try to micromanage your day from a distance. The calls," she said, holding her forehead. "They're endless! That was Mrs. Friedman. Did I know that Bonne, spelled B-O-N-N-E, Friedman, whose medical form *clearly states* she is lactose intolerant and should under no circumstances consume dairy products, ate an ice-cream sandwich on Tuesday? Why, yes, Mrs. Friedman, I am aware. At exactly twelve noon, Eastern Standard Time, I personally rammed that ice-cream sandwich down your daughter's throat. I took the Tofutti Cutie—*that she knows full well is there, that we put out especially for her and the vegans*—out of her hand myself."

Carly looked up from her laptop. She hadn't heard her mother's biting humor in what seemed like ages. Through the years at Bellwin, Isabelle had become quite the mimic, performing some of the more egregious parental atrocities for Nick and Carly's amusement at night.

"See, I wanted her to get gassy. I wanted her to fart all night and get made fun of by the girls in her cabin."

They laughed. Together. "That's good, Mom. You should write a book."

Isabelle returned her gaze back to her computer screen and kept it fixed there. "Actually, I have. A couple, as a matter of fact. No one's interested."

"I know. I know. Sorry," Carly said. Her mother had never actually invited Carly to read her fiction, but one time, when she was using her mother's computer, Carly had peeked at a manuscript. The part she had read was a long scene with a middle-aged couple hiking in the Grand Canyon, fighting about whether they were going to live in New York or California and what each place would "mean." Carly found it boring and gave up after two pages. She'd never felt the need to pry after that.

"But I mean a *funny* book. A camp director/college admissions counselor tell-all. *The Stupid Things Parents Do and Say.* Something like that. What's the deal with that Genevieve girl? The one you made Jess trade places with?"

Isabelle rolled her eyes. "Genevieve Hartmann had to be moved away from the window in her cabin. The cold air was aggravating her vocal cords, and Genevieve needs to preserve her vocal cords for the music camp she'll be attending later this summer—and, apparently, for the stardom that is her destiny."

"See. You're funny." Carly said. "That Genevieve is a brat, by the way. She never scrapes her plate. She purposely makes extra-disgusting piles of food before sending her tray in on the conveyor belt. It drives Brian nuts."

Isabelle didn't say anything. She made a sound, kind of like *hmm*, but she didn't take the opening.

When Carly was seeing Harris Gibson, Isabelle was reasonably curious. Not terribly intrusive but curious. She asked questions about where he lived, what kind of stu-

dent he was. But with Brian, she'd exhibited little to no interest after Carly told her he wasn't planning to go to college unless the music thing didn't work out. Her eyebrows
went up and her lips went in and she offered one of her
*hmm*s. But she didn't ask about the music, or his family or
anything. She had made inquiries about adult supervision
when Carly told her she was going over to Ernestine's the
first time, but she'd shown no interest in hearing anything
more.

Which was too bad, because Carly could imagine
Sheryl and Isabelle liking each other. She could see Nick
fitting right in with the family, telling stories about growing up in Queens or the early days in the Meatpacking
District. The Quinn family dinners sort of reminded her
of the dinners Nick and Isabelle used to have back when
the loft was half finished.

"Wow."

"What?"

"A lead. Two bedrooms, decent neighborhood. Affor—
Well, not *too* expensive." Isabelle reached for her phone and
pushed a button. "Come on. Come on, Nancy. Pick up."

Isabelle's sister Nancy, who lived across the river from
Manhattan in Jersey City, had been going to check out
apartments for Isabelle.

"There you are. I have a lead. You've got to go first
thing tomorrow. . . . Yes. . . . I don't know. . . . Nan, I told
you. I don't care how close it is to the PATH train."

Nancy kept trying to convince Carly's mother that Jersey City—where she had bought a condo—was not only not bad, but in some ways better than Manhattan.

"I'm not going to live in Jersey City. . . . Not even temporarily. . . ."

"So I'm going to go," Carly said as she headed toward the door.

Isabelle nodded and waved. "Look. If I have to lose Manhattan on top of everything else I've lost, I'll—"

Carly let the screen door slam over the end of that sentence and headed up the camp driveway to the road, where Brian had said they'd pick her up. He'd told her to be there by eight fifteen.

When it turned out that Val couldn't—or wouldn't—come, Brian had second thoughts about Carly going to the gig with them. "I'm not going to be able to hang with you. And those frat guys—I don't know."

But Carly really wanted to see Quinn play for an audience, and she assured him she could take care of herself.

By eight thirty she was still waiting. She didn't think Brian would stand her up. Even if he changed his mind, he'd call and tell her. But why weren't they there yet? He'd told her she couldn't be late. She took out her phone to call him but decided not to. Not yet. She didn't want to be one of those girls.

A few cars and pickup trucks passed, raising and dashing her hopes when they turned out not to be the van.

One, a tiny red convertible with an older, well-coiffed and well-dressed couple, crested the hill and slowed to a stop beside her. The woman beamed at Carly. The man scowled at the woman.

"Hi, sugar." She was tan and jeweled and smelled like the cosmetics department at Bloomingdale's. Carly wondered if the perfume overdose was the result of an impaired sense of smell or if maybe the woman was afraid it would get blown away in the MG.

"Can you tell us where Route 213 is?" The woman held out a well-worn map with various routes highlighted in assorted colors.

"I'm sorry. I have no idea. I don't live around here, and I don't drive."

Carly's response appeared to alarm the woman. "What are you doing out here all alone?" She reached for Carly's hand. "You're not hitchhiking, are you?"

"No. No. I'm waiting for friends to pick me up."

"Does your mother know where you are?"

Carly had to think about that one. She had told Isabelle, and Isabelle had nodded.

"Yes."

"Good." The woman pointed a red-lacquered fingernail to a circled spot on the map. "We're trying to get to our son's new country house, and he gave us the worst directions."

"The worst," the man chimed in.

"Would you believe he's an engineer?"

"A computer engineer, Estelle," said the man. "Nothing to do with maps. I think they did this on purpose."

"Don't be silly," said his wife.

"What silly? They told us the wrong way so we'd get lost and we wouldn't embarrass them at the big party."

"Harvey," she said, rolling her eyes. Then she leaned in and whispered conspiratorially to Carly. "He's a little sensitive since these days. Since he retired."

Just then, to Carly's relief, the boys' van appeared over the hill.

"My friends can help you."

Avery screeched to a stop, kicking up a cloud of dust.

"Hey," Brian said as he opened the front passenger-side door and hopped out. He smiled and waved at the couple and gestured for Carly to climb in.

"Hey," she said as she walked toward him. He put an arm around Carly and pulled her in for a squeeze. He smelled soapy, and his hair was wet. He was wearing an FDNY T-shirt. "These people need directions."

"We don't have time," Avery said from the driver's seat. He looked at his watch and tapped the steering wheel impatiently.

"Yeah, well," said Brian. "If someone had started loading in when he was supposed to instead of standing in front of the mirror for twenty minutes trying to get his hair just right. . . ."

"Hey. You might not think it's important. But I'm telling you—appearance matters."

"Yeah, yeah. So start earlier next time, dude. This won't take long." Brian headed toward the couple's little red car.

Carly waved to the couple and climbed into the van. There was one bucket seat for her to share with Brian. A hard rectangular guitar case was propped up against it. "Whoa, whoa," Avery said as she squeezed herself into the seat, her leg pressing against guitar case. "Watch the Strat, okay?"

"Okay," she said, even though the guitar case hadn't moved a millimeter. Brian had warned her about this. How they all got a little stressed before gigs. She'd promised she wouldn't take it personally.

Liam lifted his chin. He was squished up against a window in the back next to his drum kit. The way-back was packed to the ceiling with guitars, amps, mic stands, and what looked like miles of wire.

Avery looked in the rearview mirror. "Come on, bro, tell them anything. They're just rich old-fart Citiots."

Carly turned to look out the window and saw Brian bent over the couple's map, tracing directions with his finger. Harvey was smiling and nodding, and Estelle had a hand on Brian's arm.

Carly was glad Brian wasn't the kind of guy who would mislead an old couple like that. Thanks to Brian, they weren't going to miss the party. Their careful dressing wouldn't go to waste.

Avery revved the engine. Brian looked up and held a hand out telling his brother to chill, but Avery didn't listen. He kept pressing the gas. Liam yelled, "Bri—we gotta go."

Brian backed away from the convertible, waved, and jogged to the van. He climbed in and pulled the door shut. "Okay. They're gonna follow us, so don't go too fast."

"Dude. Are you nuts?" Avery seemed truly mad now. "We're gonna to have to book if we're gonna be set up by nine thirty."

"We'll get there."

"Yeah, well, I don't think my speed is the problem, 'cause that old man is on my ass."

"Oh yeah?" Brian looked in the side-view mirror and laughed. He rolled down the window, stuck his head out, and waved. Carly couldn't see anything from where she was, but she heard the *toot-toot* of the MG.

Avery accelerated. She watched the speedometer climb over sixty and looked over Brian's shoulder to the unused seat belt. He saw, smiled, and pulled it down across her waist. As he leaned across her to click it in, he nuzzled her neck. She was covered in goose bumps despite the heat. He didn't take his arm back after he clicked the seat belt in. She rested her hands on his forearm and closed her eyes for the rest of the ride.

- - -

After two songs, Carly understood why Brian had been reluctant to take her along. There were about two guys for every girl in the crowded yard behind the frat house and they were all on the prowl. But because she could still feel the spot on her neck where Brian had nuzzled her in the van, because she knew he'd be kissing her there and elsewhere in a matter of time, she didn't mind how guys kept coming up to her asking what year she was, if she wanted a beer, or a Jell-O shot, or to check out the Den of Iniquity in the basement.

Most left her alone after she said no. Some tried again, asking if she was sure, if maybe she brought a friend? And when they didn't get the response they wanted, they'd back off.

Except this one guy. He was pretty drunk, and he wanted to know why Carly was so unfriendly. What was she doing there if she didn't want to "interact civilly with other human beings"?

By which he apparently meant himself.

Carly told him she was with the band and he wanted to know which guy. And for some reason she told him. Then he wanted to know what a girl like her would see in "that bony-ass bass player." He said he could understand if it was that "pretty-boy singer dude."

Carly was leaning against a fence in the backyard, right next to the deck that was serving as a stage.

Brian knew she was there. When she first made her

way through the crowd and found the spot, he'd looked up and winked and waved his chin. But he hadn't looked back since. He'd warned her about this, too. He told her he had to concentrate during shows, because if he started to notice the crowd, he got all nervous and worried about what people thought about them, and then his playing would get all messed up. He kept his head down most of the time he was onstage.

So he didn't see how this guy kept moving closer, how he got so close she could smell his beery breath.

She reached into her pocket for her phone and typed out what she hoped was an understandable text to Val.

Cll now! 9-1-1.

Beer Breath stared at Brian as he leaned in and said, "I mean, he can't weigh more than one thirty."

Now she could smell hamburger and onions, too. He wanted to know if she'd ever been to a rugby game. He said rugby players were tougher than football players.

"No pads. No helmets."

"Really," Carly said. "Is that what happened?"

"Huh? What happened? What?"

"Is that how you—" It was probably a good thing that her phone rang before she could ask if he got the brain damage playing rugby. "Just a sec—this might be my dad. He's picking me up."

Beer Breath was gone before she got to the *i* in "hi."

"What's wrong?"

"Nothing. I just needed an excuse to get away from an overly friendly frat boy."

"Where's Brian?"

"Playing."

"And you're . . . ?"

"Waiting. Watching."

"Uh-huh."

"What?"

"Waiting? Watching? You've been doing that for how long?"

Carly looked at her watch: 11:14. Brian said they'll be done with their second set by midnight. "Just a couple hours. But there was a break between sets."

"*Just* a couple hours? Wow. That didn't take long."

"What didn't take long?"

"For you to turn into a groupie."

"Val. I am *not* a groupie. That's not how it is. That's not how Brian is."

"Uh-huh."

"I'm serious, Val. You don't know him." Carly thought about Estelle and Harvey, how Brian had helped them despite Avery and Liam's protests. She wished Val had been there to see that. Or how affectionate he was with his mother. And with Carly.

"Okay. Okay, I won't judge. Yet. But, I mean, what do

you expect when you tell me you're all alone at a frat party and then you send a text like that? Do you know what they call freshman girls? Freshmeat."

"That's an urban legend."

"It's not. Here, ask Luis."

"No. Val—"

As she handed Luis the phone, Carly thought she heard her say something about setting someone straight.

"Hey, Carly Girly. You hanging with the frat boys now?"

"Hey, Luis. No. I'm just—I just came to hear the guys play."

"Well, be careful. Everything you heard is true. Those boys are looking for one thing. I'm surprised your boy—what's his name?"

"Brian."

"I'm surprised Brian let you go."

"*Let* me?"

"Yeah. Let you. Don't go all *feminista* on me here."

"I won't go all *feminista* if you don't go all *machis-mista*."

"But I didn't mean *let* you like give you permission. I just meant—"

When a pair of arms suddenly circled her waist, she gasped. But then she recognized the heart-shaped freckle above the elbow and let herself sink back into the safety of Brian.

"Carly? Hey, Carly! You still there?"

"Hey, Luis. Thanks. Yeah. It's okay. Brian's here. Tell Val I'll call her tomorrow."

Carly turned toward Brian, ran her fingers through his dripping-wet hair, and planted her lips on his. The kiss was half for Brian, half for the benefit of her rugby-playing sexual harasser, in case he was watching.

"Whoa," Brian said. "Guess you're glad to see me."

"Uh-huh."

"See what I mean about these frat gigs? There are too many guys like that around here." So he had seen.

Carly shrugged. "Guys like what?"

Up on the stage, Avery and Liam were unplugging and packing and talking up the girls gathered around, phones out, fingers poised, hoping to get numbers. Another girl walked over and handed them each a red plastic cup of beer.

"You okay?"

"Yup."

He kissed her on the neck. "I'll be right back."

She held the place on her neck where he kissed her and watched as he climbed the steps to the stage and started packing. Brian worked quickly while Avery and Liam took their time, entertaining their admirers as they slowly packed their equipment. When the beer-delivery girl approached Brian, red cup in hand, Carly started to feel a little less okay. The girl leaned over, offering him the cup, a smile, and a close-up of her cleavage.

He looked. He nodded. He smiled.

Carly stopped breathing.

Brian took the cup from the girl's hand and said something that made her giggle.

She said something that made him laugh.

It went like that, back and forth a few times and then—

He waved, turned away, and started winding cables again.

The girl stood there looking at his hunched back for a few seconds, and when he didn't look up, she turned and rejoined the gaggle surrounding Avery and Liam.

Carly resumed breathing.

13

STONY HOLLOW was good for Jess. During mealtimes, whenever Carly would peek out through the conveyor-belt window, she'd see her little sister in the middle of a group of girls, laughing or singing or engaged in one of those endless clapping games that seven-year-olds do obsessively. Sometimes Jess would sneak back into the kitchen to exchange hugs with Carly and play around with Brian, Liam, and Avery, who doted on her. If Kevin wasn't around, they'd let her stand on a stool and rinse things with the overhead power washer—which, because she didn't have to do it for hours a day, she found fun. One night Liam and Avery enlisted her help in building a giant pyramid of plastic cups then knocking it to the floor.

She liked horseback riding and, unfortunately for Carly because she had to watch what she said about Cameron Foster, sailing. But of course drama was her favorite activity. She played the Undersecretary of Understanding in *The Phantom Tollbooth* and stole the show—in Carly's opinion—during the Parents' Weekend production.

Nick came up for that weekend, which was tense. He and Isabelle were stiff and awkward with each other, while pretending to be great friends. Carly just felt weird. She introduced him to Brian, and the three of them sat together for Jess's play on Saturday night, but what conversation they had never moved beyond small talk.

All summer she'd been thinking about how well Nick and Brian would get along, how much she was sure Nick would love Brian's music. She'd imagined taking Nick back to Ernestine's so he could hear the guys rehearse and see the cool old house. But when they were both there, sitting on either side of her, there didn't seem to be any point to trying to connect them when Carly's own connection to Nick was so uncertain.

Nick made an effort. He invited her and Brian to join him and Jess for dinner the next day. The kitchen crew always got Sunday afternoons and evenings off. Usually the camp bought pizza from a place in town, and the campers ate dinner in the sheltered annex down by the lake, but since it was Parents' Weekend, some families were going into town for dinner.

"Invite Brian, too," Nick said. "He can tell us where to go, and I can hear more about the band."

But Carly said no. Brian had told her he had a surprise planned for that afternoon, and she'd been invited for dinner at Ernestine's afterward. She knew that all she had to do was ask and Sheryl would insist that Nick and Jess come along. But Carly was surprised to find that she didn't want to ask. She didn't want to share Sheryl and Brian and the Quinn clan with her falling-apart family. She wanted them all to herself.

All Brian would tell her about their mystery outing was that they'd be driving part of the way in the van and walking the rest. He'd told her to wear long pants and long sleeves and good walking shoes. And he'd refused to tell her anything else.

They drove along a winding country road, past run-down houses with yards full of junk next to newly pimped-up farmhouses with swimming pools and tennis courts and shiny new Range Rovers. One of these places had a brand-new stable, red with white trim, in front of which they saw two little girls—who couldn't have been older than eight or nine—decked out in jodhpurs and boots and holding riding crops.

Now and then they'd catch a glimpse of the Hudson, which looked dark green against the clear blue late-summer sky.

Eventually Brian turned onto a dirt road. It was full of bumps. Rocks and pebbles crashed and clicked against the underside of the van.

Carly kept asking where they were going. Not so much

because she wanted to know but because she loved the sneaky smile that would appear on his face when he said "Not telling."

Finally they pulled off and parked on the shoulder. There were no other cars, but there were a lot of footprints and tire tracks. Brian pulled a small backpack from the be-hind the driver's seat, put it on, and took Carly by the hand to the edge of the seemingly endless, pathless woods.

"How will we find our way back? There's no path."

"Sure there is, if you know how to look." He reached out and pulled the branch of a small tree. A small piece of light-blue plastic ribbon hung from its end. They took a few steps past the tree to another that had a piece of that same ribbon dangling down.

"See? Like Hansel and Gretel, only no one's gonna eat these."

They followed the little blue ribbons for about fifteen minutes until they came to a small, hilly opening in the woods. What looked like part of a brick wall rose a few feet from the ground at the foot of the hill. Behind that wall—under a pile of branches and dead leaves that Brian pulled and pushed and brushed aside—were two large rectangles of plywood.

Brian slid them aside to reveal a large hole on the side of the hill. He pulled two flashlights out of his little back-pack and handed one to Carly.

They had to crouch to get themselves all the way in, then duckwalk for about ten feet to where things opened up and they could stand.

Brian pointed his flashlight at the ground directly in front of where they stood. Steps.

The light revealed five; there were more after that.

"What is this place?"

"You'll see," he said, starting down the steps. They were barely wide enough for one person. "Coming?"

Carly followed in spite of the slight claustrophobia she felt surrounded by dark, moist earth.

The steps ended at ten, and the narrow tunnel opened up into a room. Not a hole, but a room, with four walls, all made of brick, and a ceiling of logs. On one side was an archway over what must have once been a door. Stacked logs filled the opening.

It was another one of those locals-only secret places, like Baldwin Rock. No one knew for sure what the room was for originally, Brian explained. It might have been for storage, or part of an underground tunnel used for transporting goods to and from the river during the winters. For at least thirty years, since Brian's father was a kid, the townies had managed to keep it a secret among themselves and pretty much as they'd found it. The only alteration they'd done was to add a bit of ventilation using pipes. Somehow every year the pipes were cleared of whatever dirt or debris got in there over the winter.

He walked Carly over to the logs stacked under the archway. They were filled with carved initials and numbers.

"When someone brings you here for the first time, you add yourself. There's me, and Avery and Liam." He shined the light on three sets of initials: BFQ, AFQ, and LKQ '05. "And here's my dad and my uncle Michael." He moved the light down two logs to find the SOQ and MOQ '75 that belonged to Sean O'Brien Quinn and Michael O'Brien Quinn.

He pulled a Swiss Army knife out of his pack and handed it to Carly.

"Let's find a spot for you."

Later that night, after dinner with the whole family, she and Brian lay side by side on the not-so-neatly made futon on the floor of room nine, catching their breath, letting the warm summer breeze pass over them while they listened to the crickets and the bits and pieces of the Yankees game on Sheryl's kitchen radio.

This time there was no "We better stop."

And there was no call to Val to share the news. Not that night when she got back to the cabin or in the morning when she got up. Even if Val managed to say the right words this time, Carly knew her friend's voice would betray judgment. Doubt.

And she didn't want to hear it.

Maybe after a "couple nights" she'd tell. Like Val had with the news about her and Jake. But not yet. Or maybe she wouldn't tell at all. Maybe that was how it should be, something that stayed between her and Brian.

14

BEFORE SHE knew it, the summer Carly had expected to drag by slowly was coming to a close. The day after the campers and counselors went home was a Sunday, Carly's last. The next day she was heading to Ohio for what promised to be an excruciatingly boring week at her father's, and then it was back to New York, to a dubious-sounding sublet on the West Side that Isabelle had finally found.

If Brian weren't moving back to Brooklyn, if the two of them hadn't sat down at the computer and mapped out the fastest ways to get from her new apartment to theirs in Brooklyn, if she weren't already on the guest list for their first New York City gig, she'd have been miserable.

But she wasn't miserable. Nothing—except the physical distance between them—was going to change when they got back to the city.

On her last night upstate, she was invited for dinner with the whole family. She and Sheryl had one more talk in the garden before dinner.

Carly had never seen anything like the garden at Ernestine's: a huge, triangular plot with something growing on every inch it. Flowers, berry bushes, zucchini and melon vines, tomatoes, cucumbers, even a few rows of corn.

"Damn it!" Sheryl threw her wicker basket to the ground and dropped to her knees.

"What's wrong?"

"Look at this." She held up a heart-shaped leaf with holes and ragged edges. "Goddamn beetles!"

Kneeling in the dirt next to the bean poles, Sheryl examined each vine, inch by inch. "Okay, where are you guys hiding? You may as well give up now, because you *know* I'm going to find you. Do you hear me?"

"I think they probably do," Carly said.

Sheryl laughed without looking up. "Yeah. Listen to me. I've become one of those crazy gardening ladies."

Before marrying Brian's father, Sheryl had lived her whole life in Brooklyn. "My mother grew a few tomato plants in the little space we had behind our house, but nothing like this. This is like having a grocery in your backyard."

When she and the boys moved upstate, Ernestine put her to work getting the garden ready for winter.

"God, she was a smart one, that Ernestine. She was just as torn up as I was. But in a different way, because Sean was her child. Her firstborn. But she kept me from completely falling apart. Put me to work harvesting the fall stuff, getting the garden ready for winter. And then there was all the canning. She wasn't trying to get my mind off Sean. We talked about him the whole time. But in the midst of all that death, she made it so I was up to my elbows in life. Now I'm totally hooked. Just like her, I'm trying something new every year."

Over the summer, listening to Sheryl talk about her life, Carly had fallen half in love with her, too. Also with Ernestine, even though she was dead, and the generation back in Ireland—Nellie, Ernestine's mother; Auntie Maureen; and Cousin Patrick—whom she had never met, never would meet.

She was half in love with "the whole lot of them," which is one of the expressions she heard a lot hanging around the Quinns. They called those expressions Ernestineisms, little phrases Ernestine brought with her when she came to America as a teenager and passed on to her kids and grandkids along with all the stories.

How Ernestine's cousin Patrick got kicked in the head when he turned his back on a newborn calf, or how her Auntie Maureen's fiancé died when his bicycle was hit by a bus three days before the wedding, and she never recovered. How Nellie, Ernestine's mother, took her brother's place on the family fishing boat when all the boys in the village went off to fight in World War I.

"Aha." Sheryl held out her palm for Carly's inspection. In it was a small bug. Yellow, with black spots.

"I thought ladybugs were good for gardens."

"Oh, these aren't ladybugs. They're Mexican bean beetles. Distant cousin of the ladybug. The nasty branch of the family," she said to the bug before dropping it. She took a flip-flop off her foot and squashed the bug into the ground. "Last summer, they ruined my beans." She leaned over and yelled into the plant. "That is *not* happening this year."

Two hours later, they were all crowded around Ernestine's creaky kitchen table, brainstorming band names. A thunderstorm had driven them inside. A platter piled high with empty corncobs and bare chicken bones sat next to another with a pinkish-gold puddle of olive oil dotted with tomato seeds.

The booking agent who signed the band wanted them to come up with a new name. Something with a ring to it. Something people would pay attention to and remember. The one simple word "Quinn" wouldn't do.

The boys were reluctant. They all felt loyal to Ernestine for getting them started and defending them to their parents. They didn't want to lose the name she'd given them. But the guy was adamant. They'd decided that they wouldn't get up from the dinner table until they'd found a new name.

"Dingwall Scotty?" Liam had Ernestine's seed catalogue out, convinced that the perfect name could be found among the weird names of tomato varieties. And since the book was Ernestine's, a tomato band name would still be a tribute to her.

Brian and Avery shook their heads.

"Abraham Lincoln?"

Avery scoffed. Brian scowled.

"Box Car Willy?"

Carly tuned them out and looked around, wondering how it could be possible to miss a person she'd never met.

Because she was already missing Ernestine.

She understood what Brian meant when he explained why they'd always call the house Ernestine's. Everywhere you looked, you'd see her. Every chair, couch, and bed had a crocheted afghan. The week before, Sheryl had gathered them all up and arranged them by decade. Wild, fluorescent colors from the sixties, earth tones from the seventies, mauves and purples from the eighties. Then it started all over again with the wild colors in the nineties.

The kitchen drawers were full of her handmade potholders, and all over the house you'd find framed needlepoint prayers and inspirational phrases about life, lemons and lemonade, God at your side and the wind at your back. If you picked a book up off the shelf, chances are some little bit of paper would fall out, with a note about what she needed at the store, or a question about a recipe. Sometimes it was a passage she'd copied out from the book, or notes to herself ranging from the mundane—"call carpet cleaner" and "check with Michael about Monday"—to the utterly mysterious: "seventeen silver birds' nests."

They called these Ernestineabilia, and had been taping them to the wall next to the refrigerator as they appeared. It was covered in scraps of paper in varying colors and sizes, all with Ernestine's neat, schoolteacherish handwriting.

Carly didn't mean to suggest a band name when she said "Ernestine is everywhere."

But as soon as she said it, everyone stopped talking and looked at her.

Brian repeated it slowly. "Ernestine . . . is . . . Everywhere."

Liam said it faster, "ErnestineisEverywhere."

"EiE for short," Avery said.

Sheryl smacked the table. "Of course! That's brilliant, Carly. Brilliant."

15

CARLY'S WEEK in Ohio was spent helping her father transform what had been the guest room into a pink paradise for the baby. Carly had to sleep on a pullout couch in the study her father and Ann shared. The room was crammed with cases of diapers and other assorted baby gear.

She returned to New York, where home was now a fifth-floor walk-up in an uptown neighborhood, a part of town so indistinct it didn't have a name. Not even one of those that real estate agents make up to make nowhere sound like somewhere. Carly's mother tried, though. For a while she called it the "Outer Upper West Side." Then it was "Almost Morningside Heights."

Carly called it "West End of the Earth."

The only store within five blocks was a little bodega with a huge selection of chips, candy, tropical fruit juices, and beer, but little in the way of real food.

For groceries, they had to walk ten blocks to a D'Agostino on Broadway. The building had no laundry room. Washing clothes required a four-block walk, an hour and a half of sitting (longer if you had to wait for a machine), and at least ten dollars' worth of quarters.

The apartment had two small rooms: the bedroom, where her mother and Jess slept, was big enough for a bed and a small bedside table. The second room contained everything else—living room, kitchen, and Carly's room, which wasn't really a room but a corner closed off by a pair of dark blue drapes hanging by a piece of rope nailed to the wall on each end. Carly's mother got the idea from the IKEA catalogue, which was full of impossibly happy people living in impossibly small places.

The first weekend Carly was back in the city, Jess went to Nick's, and Carly went to IKEA with her mother. They bought shelves and brackets, under-the-bed drawers and hooks in almost every size the store carried.

The hooks made Isabelle optimistic about the apartment.

"We can do this," she kept saying. "A hook for everything and everything on its hook."

And, "I promise this is just temporary. I'll find us a better place."

When Nick dropped Jess off on Sunday morning, he offered to help put the stuff together and mount the hooks on the walls for them. He seemed happy when Isabelle accepted his offer, and he said he'd come back that afternoon with his tools. Carly was relieved to see that they were being civil with each other. Kind of almost even friendly.

But then after he left, her mother asked Jess about her weekend, and Jess told them about how much fun she had with Nick and his friend Chantal, how they watched a movie that included a scene with a man and a woman taking a bath together and splashing a lot of water on the floor.

Isabelle's face went white. She sat there for a second, her lips scrunched tight. Like she was deciding whether or not to ask the question. Finally she did.

"Did Chantal sleep over?"

Jess giggled. "No!"

Isabelle closed her eyes and took a long, relieved breath.

"But she came back for breakfast in the morning. She brought pastries—corrsants and—"

Before Jess could finish, Isabelle stood up, grabbed her phone, and disappeared into the bedroom. After the first "How could you?" Carly whisked Jess outside, promising a trip to the playground in Riverside Park and her choice of chips at Nuevo Mundo.

Carly and Isabelle didn't see eye to eye on much those days, but she was with her mother on this one:

How *could* he? Wasn't there, like, a mandatory waiting period before you were supposed to introduce your kid to your new girlfriend?

It wasn't just the timing, though. When Isabelle and Nick first got together, they used to fake Carly out with the coming-over-for-breakfast trick. Nick would be there when she went to bed, but not when she woke up. Then, suspiciously soon after she'd gotten out of bed, he'd suddenly show up with the newspaper and bagels, pretending to "come over for breakfast" when what he'd really done was sneak out as soon as they heard Carly stir. When the truth finally dawned on Carly a few years later, they all laughed about it together. It was their family joke.

The IKEA stuff stayed in boxes.

Most of it, anyway. Carly put together this one piece they had bought for her "room": a tall, narrow cubbyhole/shelf thing "perfect for making the most of small urban spaces," according to the catalogue.

It took her three hours. Four if she counted the ten-block search for a place to buy a screwdriver and wrench. She did her best to follow the nonverbal instructions, did everything the smiling cartoon IKEA man did, but something wasn't right. She had to prop it in the corner to keep it from falling over. Despite her efforts to even it out with folded bits of cardboard, it wobbled every time she put something away or got something out.

Isabelle's dreams of living large in small spaces seemed to fizzle after that incident. She stopped looking for apartments. She pretty much stopped cooking. And she didn't do much talking, either.

Always the professional, she still managed to get up and go to work every day, driving all the Bellwin seniors about their applications and essays as hard as she'd always done.

That was the other thing.

As the daughter of the college-placement director at the Julia Bellwin School for Girls, Carly was quite familiar with the annual collective insanity that gripped 25 percent of the upper-school population and their parents every fall.

Even though most of them hired private consultants, and even though Isabelle had a staff of associates, Bellwin parents expected Isabelle Greene, placement counselor extraordinaire, to "be there for them" and their daughters during this trying time.

College-crazed parents were the reason they had an unlisted home number and the reason Carly was under strict orders *never* to give her mother's cell number to anyone she hadn't preauthorized. One Sunday morning about three years before, Carly, Jess, and Isabelle had been accosted by Lindsey Nakashima, her mother, *and* her father when they walked out of their building on their way to the park. They'd obviously been waiting a long time. Each held a different version of Lindsey's personal statement for Harvard. The early-action deadline was the next day, and they couldn't decide whether Lindsey should go with the one about how capoeira had changed her life, or the one about her homeless friend, Nadine, whose grit and determination had opened Lindsey's eyes to the injustices of the world and the strength of the human spirit.

And yet, in spite of all she'd seen and heard over the years, Carly was still caught off guard in September when everyone around her turned into a freaked-out zombie, unable to talk about anything except "apps."

Even Val. Even though she had always made fun of the craziness before.

Carly tried not to hold it against her. Val had more to worry about than most of the other Ivy League aspirers. She didn't just need to get in; she needed financial aid. Because she would be the first generation of her family to go to college, Val was eligible for several special scholarships at the schools where she was applying. These programs often had their own separate, additional applications, so Val was doubly busy.

And then there was Jake. He was now at Cornell, but that didn't necessarily free up time. When she wasn't staring into her computer, working on the various versions of her personal statement, Val was staring at her phone, smiling at Jake's nonstop texts.

Carly and Val never talked about it explicitly, but it was clear that their friendship was changing.

Val and Brian met twice, and neither time did anything to dispel Val's assumptions about him or to convince her that he was the great, affectionate, level-headed guy Carly knew him to be.

The first time was when Carly dragged Val to a gig, one of the Thursday-night new-band showcases at Train. They could only stay until eleven, and EiE didn't go on until ten thirty, which meant that the only opportunity for Carly to introduce them was before the show, and Brian was never at his interpersonal best before a show. The pressure of performing in New York had made this even worse, and when Carly brought Val backstage to introduce them, Brian barely looked up from his bass.

He wasn't completely rude. He said "Hey, Val," and he did make eye contact with her and even smiled when he did. It wasn't like he didn't make an effort. He explained that he'd just broken a string warming up and wanted to get the new one replaced so that he could get back to warming up.

"Can you guys stick around after our set?"

But they couldn't. Angela was very strict about that stuff. It had been hard enough to get her to agree to let Val out on a school night.

Val wasn't mean about it. She told Carly she understood about how Brian got tense before a show. And she was obviously really impressed with the music. They stayed for two songs, and Val told Carly she thought the band was really good, much better than she had imagined. Maybe they did have a shot at success.

But she obviously wasn't any closer to thinking Brian was great boyfriend material.

The next weekend, Val suggested Carly invite him to the restaurant for Sunday brunch. Jake was going to be down from Ithaca for the weekend. It would be fun for all of them to get together. But it didn't happen. Or not the way it was supposed to. Brian called that morning to report that the water heater in the Brooklyn house had flooded and Sheryl needed him to find a plumber and supervise the repairs for the tenants. No one trusted Avery to handle this kind of thing. He said he'd try to make it later, but they shouldn't wait for him to eat.

So Carly sat through brunch with Val and her friendly, well-mannered boyfriend, who showed up on time, ordered in perfect Spanish, and made a point of including Carly in all their conversations. Brian showed up three hours after the brunch was supposed to start. Jake had to catch a train, so the two of them merely shook hands. When Val brought a plate of chicken stew, pink beans, and rice, Brian asked if he could have it to go. He apologized. Said it looked and smelled great and he was sure he'd love it later, but he was just too full to eat. He had gotten so hungry, he'd ordered a pizza and split it with the plumber.

After that, Carly realized she would have to give up the idea that if Val could just get to know Brian, she'd understand why Carly was so nuts about him. He missed brunch because he was a responsible son who took care of the stuff that needed taking care of. He wasn't being rude about the food. He really did like it, and later that night when he was back home in Brooklyn, he called Carly to tell her how great it was and how he had to fight Liam and Avery off for it. Carly passed that information on to Val, but it didn't appear to have much—if any—impact.

They continued to work together every Saturday night, and they still hung out together at school, but Carly and Val had less and less to talk about with each other.

Talking to Paula Castleman was no longer an option. In fact, Paula was no longer. She'd gone to Rome that summer and come back wanting to be called "Paola," the Italian version of her name, pronounced kind of, but not exactly, like "Pow-La." Every time she saw Carly and Val, she'd greet them with nonironic two-cheeked European kisses and exclaim, *"Bella! Bella!"* It was what you did in Rome.

Paula had somehow become friends with Chloe Brosnan, Bellwin's biggest junior socialite and budding philanthropist. That fall, Chloe was putting on her first very own charity ball, raising money on behalf of endangered gorillas in Africa, and she'd invited Pow-La to be on her "advisory board." From what Carly could tell, this involved difficult tasks like deciding which kinds of hors d'oeuvres to serve and what colors to choose for their theme.

All of this made Carly a lot more needy when it came to Brian. The only time she felt right was when she was with him.

But being with Brian in New York was a lot more complicated than it had been at Stony Hollow, where they saw each other every day at work and Ernestine's was a five-minute walk from the camp. Upper Manhattan and Brooklyn, though technically both part of the entity known as New York City, are pretty far apart. The fastest public transportation could bring them together was forty-five minutes, and that didn't count walking to the subway or waiting on the platform.

They stayed in almost constant electronic contact. Carly would text him when she woke up in the morning and hear back from him when he got up a few hours later. They'd exchange more texts at lunch and between classes.

But whenever they wanted to see each other live and in person, they had to figure out a time and place to meet. She couldn't see him during school hours, and he couldn't see her most nights because of practice and gigs. Plus, to make ends meet, he started working weekend days at a music store in Greenwich Village. Carly needed her Saturday-night shifts at SJNY more than ever now that her mother was watching every dollar.

All told, they probably had ten good face-to-face days in the two months they lasted past the end of summer.

That's an average of one good day a week.

And those good days really only amounted to a few hours at a time.

There was one great afternoon walk through Riverside Park; one movie-montage-worthy trip to the mummy exhibit at the Met. One cold Sunday morning in early October they took the subway out to Coney Island and drank three hot chocolates apiece while they snuggled on a bench on the boardwalk making up stories about the people walking by.

Truly private time was even harder to find. The basement apartment in the Brooklyn house only had one bedroom. Avery and Liam were nice about it, and would make themselves busy on Sunday afternoons so Carly and Brian could get a little alone time. They had one amazing night on Carly's little futon on the floor when Jess was at Nick's and Isabelle was out for dinner and a movie with her sister Nancy, and Carly felt as good as she had during the summer.

When it was just the two of them, she didn't hate the apartment. She imagined they were living there together, that she was in college and he was playing music and they were poor but happy young people in New York.

When they were alone together like that, she felt like she had during those afternoons at Baldwin Rock, or nights they sat out on Brian's roof, or on the day he took her to the secret underground room.

But as those weeks went by, another Carly emerged. This Carly was whiny, needy, clingy, and jealous. She took over Carly's thoughts, put words in her mouth, and made her do stuff she'd instantly regret but somehow couldn't stop herself from doing.

It was like being possessed.

16

THE FIRST time this happened was in October.

Ernestine is Everywhere got booked for the weekly Thursday-night showcase at Train, a club on the Lower East Side. Shira Zeidman, a drama major from LaGuardia Arts High who ran a popular indie-music blog called ShiraZ, wanted an interview. She told Brian she'd seen a lot of bands come and go, and she thought they really had something.

Liam and Avery didn't think some drama-nerd girl with a blog could do much for them, but Brian knew better. He understood that if the arty New York kids liked you, word would spread fast and no telling how far. He'd done his homework—seen how many friends and followers Shira had and knew she'd reviewed and interviewed some big bands before they'd gotten big.

He was excited about it and invited Carly to come along. So on a rainy October afternoon, they met up after school and trekked across town to Café Fortuna, where Shira used the big back booth as her office.

Carly drank tea and ate chocolate cake and listened while Brian told Shira the story of how the band was born. As well as Carly knew the story, she loved hearing it again. She loved hearing Brian talk about the place where everything started. Not just EiE, but also the two of them.

Shira asked him about the band's name and Carly sat up, waiting for him to give her props for thinking of it. She listened happily and proudly as Brian told Shira all about Ernestine, how she had encouraged the boys to pursue their music, especially after their father died. How she had made The Plan with them: pursue the music dream for a year, and if it looked like something was going to happen, keep going. If there was no progress, then back to school.

Carly waited for him to get to the part about how she came up with the name that night they all sat around Ernestine's table, brainstorming.

But he never did. He told Shira all about Ernestine's house—the funky rooms, the needlepoint, the crocheted afghans, the Ernestineisms and Ernestineabilia. But he never told her about how Carly was the first one to say "Ernestine is Everywhere."

When they left the café, she tried really hard not to ask him about it. She wanted to just be happy for them. She told herself it wasn't about her. She should be happy that the band was starting to get some buzz. It didn't matter who came up with the name. What mattered was that it was a good name. It was the right name. It wasn't like she was actually *in* the band or had written the songs or anything.

But before they'd even gotten a full block away from the café, she found herself saying, "Don't I get even a little credit?" She tried to make it sound light and jokey, but even she could hear the whiny undertone.

"Huh?"

"For coming up with 'Ernestine is Everywhere'?"

"Of course you do," he said, putting his arm around her and pulling her close. It was raining even harder now, and when he kissed her neck, he sent a trickle of water rolling down her back. "It's a great name."

"So why didn't you tell her it was my idea?" By now there was nothing under about the tone. She was flat-out whining, and she wasn't sure why.

"I didn't?" He squinted, puzzled, like he really thought he had.

She shook her head. "Nope."

"Oh, geez. I meant to, Carl. I totally meant to."

But he hadn't.

"I guess it slipped my mind. I was nervous, you know? I wanted her to like me and tell people to come see us, so I just wasn't thinking about that part of the story."

"Of course. Forget I said anything. It's not important."

"It is important. Everybody loves our name. I'm going to tell her." He pulled his phone out of his pocket.

"No! Don't do that." Now she was embarrassed. "It's silly. Just leave it." But she was glad to hear him say that it mattered to him. And she was glad that he ignored her protests and typed out a text.

"Too late," he said with a smile as he shut the phone and put it back in his pocket. "It's done."

Carly stayed up that night, hitting Refresh on Shira's blog over and over until the interview showed up.

ShiraZ

ERNESTINEISEVERYWHERE

If you've been at any of the new-music showcases at Train recently, you've probably been wondering, as have we, why you never heard of Ernestine is Everywhere before. You're probably also wondering when you'll get to see these guys headlining, instead of playing a few songs jammed between amateurish wannabes. The guitar-bass-and-drums trio, made up of Brooklyn-born brothers Brian and Avery Quinn and their cousin Liam Quinn, has spent much of the last five years writing songs and working on their quirkily arranged '80s covers locked in a shed behind their grandmother's house upstate.

Okay, maybe not locked. But the door was closed, and no one was allowed in.

Their grandmother's name was—anyone?—Ernestine,

of course, and the boys credit her with giving them the inspiration to pursue their music seriously. "She was amazing," says bassist and songwriter Brian. "When we moved in with her, she gave us the shed and told us to get to work. She had it wired for electricity, and our mother let us spend all our time back there." Their name, suggested by a family friend, is tribute to her influence.

A family friend?
What did that mean?

Is that what Brian texted her? Or were those Shira's words? She couldn't ask him. Not after whining like she had that afternoon. And she couldn't ask Shira. That would be totally weird.

Her doubts should have been put to rest a few days later, when Brian invited her out to Brooklyn for the boys' first attempt at putting on a Quinn family Sunday-night dinner without Sheryl there to cook. Avery had gone up to Ernestine's the day before, and Sheryl sent him back with a batch of her special spaghetti sauce—made with the last of the summer tomatoes—and step-by-step instructions for re-creating her garlic bread.

When Carly got there, she found the three of them laughing it up in the kitchen. Brian stood at the stove warming sauce, boiling water, and assembling the garlic bread; Avery and Liam sat at the table, each with a laptop in front of him. Ever since Shira's interview, they'd been bombarded with new friend requests, most of them from girls, and a lot of them offering more than cyber friendship.

Avery and Liam were into it. Big-time. One by one they would check out every girl wanting to friend them. They didn't reject anybody. That would be bad business. But if a girl looked hot, they might strike up a messaging relationship.

Avery started going a little nuts, promising all these girls he'd put them on the guest list, inviting them backstage, taking their cell numbers.

Brian didn't approve.

"Whoa. Whoa. Hold on. Only real girlfriends go on the guest list."

"Dude. That's not fair. You're the only one with a 'real girlfriend.' We're supposed to just let all these opportunities fly by?"

"Dude. Do you know how many psychos are out there?"

Avery looked at Liam and smiled. "Psycho isn't necessarily a bad thing."

"Yeah," Liam laughed. "There's 'Woo-hoo, let's party' psycho, and there's 'Hi, I'm going to seem fun and wild at first, but then I'm going to get scary and start stalking you' psycho."

"My point exactly," Brian said, as he lifted the pasta pot

from the stove and carried it to the sink. Carly watched his biceps expand as he poured the spaghetti into the colander, rejoicing in the affirmation of her status as girlfriend, hoping they'd get some time alone after dinner. "So don't you think we should have some standards? Some kind of limit on who we put on that list?"

"Okay, does this girl look like a psycho?" Avery walked over to the stove, holding the screen of his laptop out for Brian to see. A blonde girl in a lacy black bra gazed seductively into her webcam, puckering her lips.

Brian laughed. "Yeah, as a matter of fact she does."

The question about how to manage the guest list consumed the dinner conversation. Brian agreed to give up the "only real girlfriends" idea, and Liam and Avery agreed that they'd each put only one girl on per show, and only after meeting her in person and establishing that she wasn't "an obvious psycho."

Because you couldn't always tell at first.

That conversation should have put Carly's mind to rest

It didn't matter what Shira Zeidman said or thought, or what people who read her blog thought. It mattered what Brian thought. And now she'd heard it in no uncertain terms. She was his girlfriend.

His real, guest-list-worthy girlfriend. The *only* real girlfriend among the Quinn boys.

And so why in the world would she even think about picking up his phone a little while later when she thought he couldn't see her and scrolling through his sent-message box to find that text he'd sent to Shira a few days before?

This was the night of what would turn out to be the final game of the World Series, and everyone expected the Red Sox—the Yankees' archenemies—to sweep the Colorado Rockies. Brian refused to watch, so he and Carly were in the bedroom watching a DVD while Avery and Liam followed the game in the living room. After some big play they called to Brian, demanding that he come and watch the replay.

It wasn't premeditated. It was barely even meditated. It just kind of happened. She was looking around his room idly, thinking how different it was from room nine at Ernestine's. Smaller and darker, with a slight musty basement smell coming from the old green carpet. When she looked at the carpet she saw the phone lying next to the futon, practically within reach. All she had to do was scoot over and stretch out her arm, and she'd know what he said in that text.

She didn't even get to Wednesday's messages before he walked in on her, saying, "So we should probably think about getting you ho—"

If she hadn't gasped and shut the phone as soon as she

heard his voice, her lie probably wouldn't have seemed so obvious.

"Just checking the time," she said. But she said it way too fast. And too high-pitched. "I was thinking the same thing. It's getting late."

Brian stood there for a moment, head cocked to the side, like he was thinking something over. Carly was sure he was going to ask her what she'd really been doing with his phone. But then he didn't. He just said, "Yeah. Underground is just where I wanna be when that game ends."

She decided she had to confess. And so in one long, messy blurt delivered somewhere under the East River, she told him how she'd been obsessing over Shira's interview, wondering whether he was the one who used the phrase "family friend" and what that said about how he saw her.

"Is that how you think of me, as a 'family friend'? Don't we have something more than that going on here?"

She knew as soon as she heard herself saying these things that she was ruining it. The look on Brian's face— a combination of perplexed and annoyed—was one she hadn't seen before, and she didn't like it. Up to then, she'd managed to keep her growing insecurity inside the privacy of her own head. Now that she'd spoken it out loud, it just sounded crazy.

He hadn't even noticed that Shira called her a "family friend," and he didn't get why it mattered so much to Carly. "You *are* a family friend. What's so bad about being a family friend, anyway? You're my girlfriend and you're a family friend."

"I know. I totally love your family. It's just—all these girls suddenly coming out of the woodwork—"

"I don't even *see* those girls. I mean, I *see* them. I know they're there. And believe me, I'm glad they're there, listening to us, dancing to our music. If we don't have fans, we don't go anywhere. But I'm not into the rock-star stuff, Carl. You know that. I don't care about it like those guys do. You really don't have to worry. I wish you would relax."

Carly wished she would, too. Wished she could. But it was impossible. From then on, the more popular they got, the more anxious and obsessive she got.

Soon they were playing Friday nights at Train, sharing the bill with just one other band instead of five. Kids from schools all over town stood on line to see them. Not just high-school kids, either. Some came from Columbia, NYU, and even Fordham, in the Bronx. They came knowing the words to songs and shouting requests.

The online friend and fan counts went from the hundreds to the thousands. Most of them girls, most clamoring for Avery's attention. But some wanted Brian's.

And he was truly oblivious.

Carly wasn't.

At night, in her curtained-off corner on West End of the Earth, she'd spend hours online, looking at the

girls who left messages for him. She knew it was a ridiculous way to spend her time, especially as her schoolwork
started to pile up, but she couldn't help herself.

She'd study their profiles and look at their pictures,
trying to measure the threat level. She'd comb through
their comments, looking for signs of boyfriends and to
make sure Brian wasn't friending them back.

Of course he wasn't. He truly didn't care.

One night on the phone, she let slip what she'd been
doing. She made a stupid joke about how many girls were
trying to get his attention online.

"What? Why are you looking at them?"

She laughed and lied. "Oh, I was just messing around
tonight after my homework."

Instead of her homework was more like it.

And make that every night that week.

She promised herself she'd stop. And she tried. But she
failed. Anytime she did anything on her computer, she'd
look. She'd start out with the intention of only working on
her history paper, and before she knew it, she'd be madly
Googling and scrolling and clicking.

Shows became torture. Self-inflicted torture. She'd be
okay for the first few songs, rocking out, enjoying the show
like everyone else, feeling proud of them and happy for
them.

But then she'd catch a glimpse of some girl dancing in

front of Brian. And she'd stop listening. She'd study his face, looking for the slightest sign of interest. He'd loosened up onstage since they started gigging in New York. Now he would sometimes look up and make eye contact with the audience. Sometimes he'd smile, or lift his chin at a girl. It was never anything more than that, and he was never anything more than casually friendly when girls tried to talk to him while Carly was by his side. He'd always keep an arm around her waist, or hold her hand.

Still, it made her crazy.

When the end came, Brian said all the usual stuff about how it wasn't Carly's fault.

But it was.

Of course it was.

She ruined everything.

It happened soon after she admitted her online sleuthing. Carly went backstage after their set at Train and saw him talking to a girl she had seen watching him during the show. Carly had noticed this girl in particular because she looked older than most of the other kids. Plus, she didn't seem to be with anyone. She'd spent the whole time leaning against a wall, watching the band, her eyes lasered in on Brian. This had made Carly even more suspicious than usual.

Brian didn't see Carly enter the room, so she took a couple steps back, hid behind the doorway, and watched the two of them. It looked intense. The girl had a lot to say, and she kept touching his upper arm. More than touching, it seemed to Carly. She'd put her hand out and keep it there while she talked and talked and talked. He was obviously paying close attention, nodding and smiling a lot. And he had a lot to say to her, too. More than Carly had seen or heard him say to any of the other girls who talked their way backstage after shows.

When the girl took out her phone and handed it to him, obviously for his number, Carly lost it.

She walked up to where they were standing, squeezed herself between them, took Brian's hand, and looked the girl in the eye.

"Hi," she said, in a way she hoped conveyed *back off*. "I'm Carly. Brian's girlfriend."

"Oh, hey." The girl smiled, looked warily at Brian, then at Carly, then at their hands. Carly was holding on tight; Brian's fingers were stiff and unyielding.

"So, I'm gonna go," said the girl, gesturing over her shoulder and stepping sideways toward the door. "You'll call me?" She held her extended thumb and pinky to her ear and mouth.

"Definitely," Brian said, smiling, as she headed toward the door.

When she passed through it, his smile disappeared and he pulled his stiffened fingers away from Carly's.

"What the hell was that?"

"I'm sorry. I'm just— These girls—"

"Do you have any idea who *that* girl was?"

"No."

"That was Tori Michaelson, head of A&R for Up All Night Records. She wanted to tell me how much she liked the show. She's bringing her boss in next week. She thinks she might be able to interest him in signing us."

"You're kidding! That's great!" Carly threw her arms around him, but he pulled away. He put his hands on her shoulders, held her at arm's distance and uttered those four awful words:

"We

need

to

talk."

Carly panicked. "I'm sorry," she blurted. And babbled, "I'll calm down, I promise."

He shook his head. Looked down at his feet, took a deep breath, and looked back into her eyes.

When he opened his mouth to speak, she cut him off, as if that would keep him from saying it. "I know I've been really hyper." She reached up to her shoulders, and put her hands on top of his. "It's just the transition. We're still figuring out how to be us in this new place."

He pulled his hands out from under hers and folded his arms in front of his chest. "Listen, Carly. There isn't going to be an us. Not anymore."

"But—"

"We had a great summer thing. We had a blast together. But I can't give you what you need right now. I have to focus. I have to make sure we don't blow whatever's happening here. Those guys seem to think it's all about the party." He tilted his head toward the side of the room where Liam and Avery were basking in the admiration of three girls apiece.

"You can focus. You can totally focus." With each word that left her lips, Carly knew she sounded more desperate. She *was* more desperate. But the words just kept coming. "I'll back off. We'll take a break. I should be focusing more, too."

He shook his head and said, "Things have gotten too intense."

He meant she had gotten too intense.

He said, "I need to spend more time on the music."

He meant he needed to spend less time with her.

He said it wasn't her.

But it was her.

It was totally her.

And she was just getting started.

17

SHE DIDN'T cry and she didn't tell anyone.

Not Val. Not her mother.

Why go through all that when she knew it was just temporary? Neither of them fully approved of Brian, either, and she didn't want to hear what they might say if they thought he was out of her life.

Besides, he couldn't be out of her life.

Carly was sure that if she calmed down and gave Brian some breathing room, they'd be fine. In fact, she decided, a break was a good thing; it would make their connection even stronger, their relationship better than ever, once they got back together.

And they would get back together, she was certain.

She went home that very night and started working on her senior history project, the twenty-page paper that was supposed to be the "intellectual culmination" of the Bellwin Experience. She'd decided on the Triangle Shirtwaist Factory Fire of 1911, which she'd learned about in her junior seminar on the history of New York. One hundred forty-six people—most of them girls not much older than she—died because the factory owners used to lock them in during working hours, to make sure no one could leave early or steal anything.

She had a bunch of library books sitting on the floor next to her bed and a list of Web sites to visit. She went on autopilot, digging into the reading and taking notes. When thoughts of what had transpired earlier threatened to interrupt her concentration, she willed them away. She simply refused to listen to the echoes of his "We need to talk" or "Things have gotten too intense" reverberating through her head. When her arms, of their own accord, recalled exactly how it felt when he pulled away from her hug, she typed faster.

She typed until she fell asleep and dreamed of being trapped in a burning building.

The next night, she worked her regular Saturday-night shift at SJNY and when Val asked about Brian, Carly told her he was fine, and that the band was spending some time upstate playing frat parties and recording at Ernestine's. By then they were mostly avoiding the subject of their boyfriends, so when Carly changed the subject to Val's college and scholarship applications, she was off the hook.

One night during this time her father called, deliriously happy, to report that Carly's second little sister,

Allison Elaine Finnegan, aka Ally, had been born.

"I'm sending you a picture. Right now," he said, in a voice that was both ragged and ecstatic. "You won't believe how much she looks like you." When Carly opened the picture on her laptop, she had to agree. If it weren't for her father's receding hairline and the crows' feet around his eyes, she might have mistaken the picture of him holding Ally for one of her own just-born baby pictures. From then on she got daily—sometimes hourly—pictorial updates from her father. Ally leaves the hospital, Ally rides in a car for the first time. Ally squinches up her face in something resembling a smile but is probably just gas.

Her father's excitement was over the top, yet endearing. And for a little while, the updates helped distract Carly from the misery she was resolutely avoiding.

She put some time into her application essay for Denman.

But Brian's sudden and complete absence left a huge void in her life, and no amount of baby-gazing or research or writing could fill it.

She missed him terribly. In those moments when she couldn't concentrate on her paper or admissions essay, she'd click through pictures from the summer, with Ernestine is Everywhere music blasting on her iPod. She had a bunch of pictures from Baldwin Rock; another bunch she'd taken from the lumpy armchair in the corner of the shed at Ernestine's of the guys rehearsing or goofing around for the camera. Her favorite was one she'd snapped of Brian asleep in room nine the night after their trip to the secret underground room. His face was completely relaxed, and there was a little smile on his lips.

That smile and all the pictures were proof of what they'd had together, how much she'd meant to him, how happy they *both* had been and would be again.

Then there were his old texts. Her phone could hold 400, and she'd saved every one of the 271 he'd sent. She reread them all, the best ones several times.

She kept tabs on the band, setting up a Google news alert for "Ernestine is Everywhere" and checking Shira Zeidman's blog once a day. Shira was a better updater than Avery, who kept the band's pages. That's how she heard about their being signed.

ShiraZ

ERNESTINEISEVERYWHERE

No one who reads this blog regularly will be surprised by our excitement over the news that EiE has signed a two-CD deal with Up All Night Records. Smart move, Up All Night people! I personally talked to spokeswoman Tori Michaelson at Friday night's show. She tells me recording will begin this spring, and that they're hoping for a fall release. A limited (East Coast) tour is a possibility. Ms. Michaelson promises ShiraZ readers an early preview. So be sure to check in regularly for more EiE news.

This was huge. Their dream. What they'd been working so hard for all this time. There was no way Carly could not congratulate him. Not just him, but all of them. It was the friendly thing to do.

For two weeks she'd successfully resisted the urge to call or text Brian. She figured a simple, casual, and relaxed message couldn't hurt. She composed a one-word, one-screen text:

Congrats!
xx, (2all). C

It took him a while—forty-three and a half hours—but he responded.

She was on a bus on her way home from school when her phone announced a text from Brian. Even though she'd been waiting and obsessively checking for messages, she jumped when heard the personalized ringtone he'd composed one night back at Ernestine's when they were sitting out on the roof, so she'd always know when a text was from him. It worked on her like a bell on Pavlov's dogs. As soon as she heard the first three notes, her heart started pounding. She clicked on the message and found:

Thx!

Carly took it as a good sign. Those three letters—plus the friendly exclamation point!—gave her hope. It wasn't exactly *I miss you and can't stand being alive without you by my side.* But it wasn't *go away forever,* either.

The lines of communication were open, Carly told herself. And where there was communication, there was hope. She didn't notice how much this sounded like something out of her mother's collection of self-help books.

Encouraged, she decided to wait a week longer, and then try a face-to-face. She would drop by String, the music store in the Village where he worked Saturdays. It would be a casual visit, a "happened to be in the neighborhood, stopping to say hi" pop-in. He would see that Carly could be normal, that she had a life outside of him. She wouldn't make a scene, beg him to take her back, or anything like that. She would just pop in and pop out.

And she really would happen to be in the neighborhood. She'd been planning, ever since she'd decided to write about the Triangle Fire, to visit the site. Not that there was much to see. Only a plaque on the side of a building that now belonged to NYU. But it was just a matter of blocks from String.

She wasn't exactly sure how they were going to get from "Hi, I was in the neighborhood and thought I'd stop by" to back together with a clean slate, but she figured the details would work themselves out over time. The important thing was for Brian to see that the clingy, needy, jealous person he'd seen wasn't the real Carly.

It didn't go as she'd imagined.

When she got there, he was in the back, in the glassed-off room where customers could try out instruments, helping a young girl—she was maybe eleven, twelve—and her father test out electric guitars.

Sampson, the big, dreadlocked store owner, was at the counter, doing something at the computer. "Hey, Carly. Long time no see."

Carly could tell by the way he nervously glanced back at Brian in the demo room that he knew something.

The question was, what? Carly hadn't told a soul about what she was sure was just a temporary breakup. What had Brian told people?

"Hey, Sampson." She tried to sound casual, and she might have been succeeding until she actually said the cheesy words, "I was just in the neighborhood and I thought I'd stop by."

"Oh, yeah? What brings you down here?"

"I'm doing a paper on the Triangle Fire."

The look on his face told her two things: he had no idea what the Triangle Fire was and he didn't believe her.

And so she stupidly started rattling off facts: the number of girls who died, how the doors were locked to keep them from leaving before their shift was over, how a lot of them jumped out the window rather than burn.

He nodded, like he was humoring her. Like he knew better.

As she was talking to Sampson, she kept an eye on Brian and so she saw his face when he realized she was there. He did a double take. She raised her hand in a tentative wave and smiled.

He didn't smile. His eyes didn't light up. He didn't even wave back. He just turned away and kept talking to his customers.

After a while he walked the girl and her father out of the demo room. The girl was cradling a shiny red guitar in her arms, beaming.

He wouldn't look at Carly. "Hey, Sampson. So Hayley here's decided on the Squier Fat Strat."

"Ex-cell-ent choice. Excellent choice, young lady. 'A double deadly tone machine with rock-star looks' from the fine people at Fender. Come right over here, Dad. I presume you're buying?"

"Thank you," said the dad to Brian, reaching out for a

handshake. "Thank you so much for your help."

"No problem," Brian said. Then he pointed at the beaming girl. "Good choice. Come back and show me what you learn in a couple months, okay?"

She looked at the floor, blushing. "Okay."

When he turned to look at Carly, the smile disappeared. He stepped aside, holding the door open, and nodded for her to come into the demo room.

"What are you doing here?"

"I just wanted to stop in and say hi. I was in the neighborhood. I'm doing a paper on the Triangle Factory fire in 1911. Did you know that was right around here?"

"No, I didn't."

"Yeah. Over near Washington Square—"

"Carly—I don't think it's a good idea for us to—"

"I just wanted—"

The heavy glass door swung open. It was the guy who just bought the guitar for his daughter.

"Hey," Brian said, smiling his broad Brian smile. "What's up? Everything okay?"

"Yeah," the father said. "We forgot the name of your band." He lowered his voice, "My daughter was too shy to come in herself."

The girl stood on the other side of the door, looking down at her feet. Brian walked over, tapped on the glass. When she looked up, he gestured for her to come back.

Carly slipped out the door as she walked in.

18

CARLY LEFT String mortified. Humiliated. Denial had disguised itself as hope and made a fool of her.

She forgot all about going to the Triangle Factory site and spent the rest of the day crying, slowly making her way all the way uptown on foot for work that night at SJNY.

Now that she'd been face-to-face with Brian again, she had to accept the truth. Instead of lighting up at the sight of her, Brian had recoiled.

She had to face it. She knew she had to face it. The first thing she had to do was tell Val. She would swallow her pride. She wouldn't just tell Val about the breakup; she'd tell her everything. About how she'd been obsessively reading his old texts, listening to his songs over and over, clicking through the pictures again and again. She wouldn't hold back anything.

Val would set Carly straight. Save her from herself.

- - -

As soon as she got to Val's room, she spilled the whole sad story.

"Oh, yeah," said Val. "We've got to nip this thing in the bud."

"I think we're well past the bud stage. This is more like full bloom."

"Yeah, okay. Whatever we want to call it, it ends to-night. I am not letting you turn into another Katrine."

After they'd both showered and dressed for work, Val made Carly erase all the texts and pictures on her phone right then and there. She said Carly had to do it while she was motivated. Carly wanted Val to do it for her, but Val refused.

"Uh-uh. You gotta hit that button yourself. It's part of the healing process."

Val stood over Carly with her blow-dryer. If Carly so much as slowed down, if she looked like she was getting ready to read one of the texts or study one of the pictures, Val would blast her with hot air until she picked up the pace.

"Uh-uh. Delete. Delete. Delete. That boy is taking up too much rent-free space in your head and it is eviction time."

"But—"

"No buts. Delete. Delete. Delete. His number, too."

They couldn't delete the music or pictures from the

iPod without Carly's computer, so they agreed that the next day, they'd do it by phone. Carly would call Val, and Val would talk her through those.

When they went downstairs, Val made Carly tell Luis the news. She said this was also part of the healing process. If Carly didn't tell people, it would be too easy for her slip back into her old ways.

When Carly had to say it out loud to him, the tears started all over again.

"God, I'm such a mess."

"Don't worry," said Luis. "I was a mess after Katrine and I broke up."

"You were not."

"Yeah, I was. I didn't show a lot of it in public, but I was."

"But you broke up with her."

"Yeah, so?"

"So usually it's the dumpee who's a mess."

"You think he's not upset, just because he did the breaking up? I broke up with Katrine, sure. But it's not like I stopped thinking about her. You don't stop caring just like that. I'm sure Brian still thinks about you."

Carly hoped he wasn't thinking about her right then, because she knew that if he was, he wasn't thinking good thoughts.

Sitting at the bar with Luis, with the truth out there for all to see, Carly felt calm. The grief was there. Her eyes were hot, and she had that exhaustion that comes after a day of tears. But she knew she'd be okay. She hadn't realized just how hard she had been working to keep her secret. She was glad she'd told Val and Val had made her tell Luis. With Val's support she could face the truth. It was a breakup, not a hiatus. People went through them all the time. Val was right: people lived.

"¿*Valeria?*" Angela called from the podium by the front door. "*Ven. Vente aquí y escúchame. ¡Ahora mismo!*"

"*Un momento, mamá.*" Val slid off the barstool.

Luis said, "You shouldn't worry, you know. There'll be other guys."

"I'm not worried." It hadn't even occurred to Carly to worry about whether or not there'd be other guys.

"Good."

Val rushed back and breathlessly announced—repeating Omigod and *Dios mío*—that Bernie Williams—the former Yankee center fielder and pride of Puerto Rico—was coming in for dinner that night.

Val threw her arms around Carly. "He's going to sit in with the band!"

The first thing Carly thought when she heard this news was how the Quinn family loved Bernie Williams. Especially Sheryl. Until she spent the summer hanging around the Quinn family, Carly had been only vaguely aware of Bernie Williams. She knew who he was, of course. You couldn't live in New York and not have a passing acquaintance with the

Yankees' roster. Thanks to Val she even knew that Bernie Williams was Puerto Rican, despite the misleading name. But she hadn't known anything about his music. And then all summer long, whenever they were losing a tough game, Sheryl would put his CD on at full volume and dance around Ernestine's kitchen. She said it brought them good luck. Sometimes—about half the time—it did.

Now Bernie Williams was coming to SJNY.

Sheryl needed to know this. She and Carly were friends, right? And a friend would let a friend know if there was a possibility of meeting her idol, right? Carly could reserve a table for Sheryl, and she could drive down from New Paltz in a couple hours.

"Really? Wow. What time?" Carly stood up and turned toward the ladies' room, her phone in hand.

"Not till late. Ten o'clock," Val said.

Good, Carly thought, *she'll have time to get here.*

From a stall in the ladies' room, she called Ernestine's. That number had escaped Val's notice. As she counted the unanswered rings, she imagined Ernestine's cluttered kitchen. Empty. With the old-style yellow wall phone sending its ring through the big empty house.

There was no answer, and so she left a breathless message for Sheryl and told her to call back if she wanted Carly to try to hold a table for her.

Angela was strict about phones at SJNY. A sign by the

podium and a note on the menu asked customers to silence theirs and take any conversations outside. She said it would be totally tacky for her staff to be checking messages or texting or whatever while they were supposed to be taking care of customers. Employees weren't even supposed to carry their phones at work. That way they wouldn't be tempted.

Most nights Carly and Val left theirs in a cabinet in the coatroom.

But that night, when it came time to put their phones away and Val offered to take Carly's, she said she'd do it herself, making an excuse about needing to check with her mother about picking up Jess the next day.

All night long, while people around her were enjoying themselves and each other and the music, all she could think about was whether Sheryl would call back.

Every chance she got, Carly called Ernestine's again. From the linen closet, the walk-in fridge, the coatroom.

Sheryl never picked up the phone.

It was closer to eleven when Bernie and his entourage arrived, and by then SJNY was completely packed. The dining room was full, the bar was five deep, and there was a line out the door. The band, Los Postizos, already had a huge following both in New York and in San Juan. Somehow word that Bernie Williams was going to play with them spread through uptown Manhattan and over to the Bronx, and it seemed like all of Spanish-speaking New York had come out for the party.

As Angela led Bernie through the dining room to his table, the place went nuts. People stood up. The band broke into a fast and funky, Latin-jazz version of "Take Me Out to the Ball Game," complete with congas, bass, guitar, and a full horn section.

A lot of New Yorkers go out of their way to be unimpressed by celebrity—or to appear unimpressed because they like to think of themselves as celebrities waiting to happen. They think living in the city places them above the ordinary citizens of the world. If one of those New Yorkers passes, say, Scarlett Johansson on Fifth Avenue, he'll check her out, for sure. And he'll probably tell his friends about it later, but he won't let his excitement show out there on the street. And he'd never ask for an autograph.

At SJNY nobody was pretending to be unimpressed. People kept a respectful distance—after all, the man hadn't even sat down yet. But no one was playing it cool. Bernie Williams was in the house, and the house was very, very happy.

Except Carly. Carly was miserable.

All around her, people were clapping, dancing, waving, throwing kisses, snapping cell-phone pictures. She was standing against a wall with her hand resting on her phone, her eyes locked on the door, hoping. If you'd asked her then, she would have told you that all she was hoping for was that Sheryl would get a chance to meet her idol. She believed it herself. But of course what she was hoping for was that not just Sheryl but the whole lot of them would show up and it would be like it was before.

Before she ruined everything.

There was one brief moment when she felt like she was actually at the party and not watching it on TV. It was close to midnight. Bernie was up onstage with the band, and the whole restaurant had turned into one giant dance floor.

Val came over, smiling and holding her hands out, insisting Carly dance with her. Reluctantly, Carly put her hands in Val's and let herself be pulled away from the wall. As she followed Val's lead—shook her hips and shimmied her shoulders—she experienced a few blissful moments of freedom. She felt the music traveling through her body and stopped looking at the whole thing as something Brian was missing, something that would be a hundred times better if Brian were by her side. When Val lifted her arm and twirled Carly once, twice, three times around, Carly's phone came flying off the waistband of her skirt. It clattered across the floor, landing at Angela's feet.

"Oh. Wow. I totally forgot I had that," she mumbled as she rushed to pick it up.

She would soon lose track of her lies, but that one,

to Angela, felt creepy. Angela had always been so nice to Carly. She gave her the job, and let her work as much or as little as she wanted. Angela didn't even notice the phone or hear Carly's lie. The music was too loud, and she was too distracted.

Later that night, Carly's phone vibrated as she lay half sleeping on the pullout in Val's room. She'd turned off the ringer so if Sheryl called back she wouldn't wake Val.

Her heart sank when she saw BRIAN on the caller ID. This couldn't be good.

He didn't even say hello. "You called my mom?"

"Um. Yeah," she whispered, hoping not to wake Val, hoping he'd take the hint and lower his voice, too. "Did she tell you why?"

"I know why you said you called her." He didn't lower his voice. If anything, it got louder. "I know you called her eight times."

Carly rolled off the bed, holding the phone to her chest to muffle the sound as she stumbled across Val's room and down the hall to the bathroom. Eight? Could she really have called eight times?

She turned on the light, closed the bathroom door, and sat on the cold tile floor with her back against the door.

"She wasn't home. I just kept trying because—"

"She was home, Carly. We were all home. We all heard."

When she'd called, she'd imagined the old phone's

retro ring echoing through dark, empty rooms. Across the room, on the desk where Sheryl kept her computer, they had a more contemporary phone, complete with caller ID and an answering machine. But Sheryl always kept that phone's ringer off, because she liked the sound of the old one. She said it reminded her of Ernestine.

"You were there?"

"Yup. Drove up after work. It's her birthday, and we were having a little family party before our gig at Pi-Ep, and we had to turn all the phones off because you wouldn't stop calling and what I want to know is—"

Carly pictured that scene. All three of the boys, plus Liam's parents, sitting around Ernestine's table, listening to her squealing message. She cringed as she imagined the looks exchanged, the eyes rolled, the elbows dug into Brian's side.

"—am I going to have to change my number? And my mom's, too?"

"No. Of course not."

"First you come by my work."

"Brian, I—"

"Then you call my mom? Come on, Carly. You don't want to be that girl, do you? That's not you."

"No. I don't—I'm not—I wasn't—I just wanted to tell Sheryl about Bernie Williams, that's all."

"Okay. So why not just leave a message? Why'd you keep calling?"

"'Cause you know how sometimes you come home and you forget to check your messages, and I just—I know how much she loves him and I honestly thought she'd want to know. . . . But I guess I lost count. I'm sorry."

As it turned out, it was a good thing Sheryl didn't make the trip. Carly wouldn't have been able to get her any nearer to Bernie Williams than across the room. Angela and Pedro did some serious crowd control.

"Carly—"

"Yeah?" She braced herself for more harsh words. She didn't blame him for being pissed. She'd called eight times. During Sheryl's birthday party. After doing that stupid stop-by that afternoon.

"It's nice that you thought of my mom. You know her well." He laughed. He laughed! "The woman loves her some Bernie Williams."

Carly laughed, too, relieved that he didn't seem so mad anymore. "Yes, she does."

"You know, if it wasn't a two-hour drive, I think she would have bolted the minute she heard."

"Really?"

"Yeah. But it wasn't exactly practical, you know?"

"Yeah. I guess. I wasn't thinking it through."

It was nice. Talking calmly like that. She had to concentrate, though, to keep her mind from going past *This is nice* to *Maybe* . . . It was hard, but she did it. She sat there, quietly, just breathing. Trying to accept how things were.

"You still there?"

"Yup," she said, smiling. He was being so nice. It felt so much like before.

"So, Carl?"

And he was calling her "Carl," like he did that summer.

"Yeah?" *Don't hope*, she told herself. He's just being nice.

"I wasn't planning to tell you this yet, but—it seems like the right thing to do."

Uh-oh. The blood in her ears started pounding, so she couldn't really hear what he said next. The first two words were muffled, but she heard the third and fourth loud and clear. They were *someone* and *else*.

"What?"

"I'm only telling you because I have this idea like you think maybe we're going to get back together, and you need to know—"

No, she didn't. She really didn't need to know, and she wished he would stop, but he didn't.

"I'm seeing someone else."

19

CARLY WENT back to bed, but there'd be no more sleep for her that night. It never occurred to her that he would get involved with someone else so soon. It had been only three weeks since they broke up! Who could it be? What about needing time for the music? Was it that record-company girl? Maybe he was just with her to get the record deal.

Somehow, as skanky as it would have been of him to hook up with someone for the sake of getting signed, this idea comforted her. If that was the case, at least then she'd know it wasn't real. Not in the sense of being truly together and connected like she and he were. He wouldn't be taking this new girl to the secret room.

He couldn't exactly bring someone like that home to Sheryl, could he? Had he? Had he brought whoever she was home? Had the new girl been sitting there, celebrating Sheryl's birthday with them? Had she heard Carly's messages and rolled her eyes, too?

She looked over at Val, who was sound asleep with a little smile on her face. Probably dreaming about Jake. She couldn't tell Val what Brian had just told her. That would mean admitting that she'd called Sheryl just minutes after promising she'd avoid all things Brian. It would be humiliating.

As she lay there wide awake, Carly's fingers itched for Val's laptop. Now that she knew, she needed to know more. She needed to know who this "someone" was who had replaced her so quickly.

Maybe that was the real reason she didn't want to tell Val. Val would be keeping an eye on Carly now. Now that she'd heard all the gory details of Carly's obsessing over Brian, she'd be on the alert, watching for signs of relapse.

When the sky finally lightened at about six, Carly rolled off the pullout and crept out of the apartment.

She couldn't remember the last time she'd been up this early on a Sunday morning. The streets of New York are never so quiet as they are at that hour. Almost every store she passed was closed, with its security gate down and locked. She saw the early shift of green-aproned baristas getting the Starbucks between Val's place and hers ready to open. She saw dressed-up old ladies climbing the steps in front of St. Cecilia's, and a disheveled guy in a tux emerging from that new luxury high-rise on Lexington.

Carly knew exactly what she had to do to get the information she needed. When she got home, she opened her computer, went straight to Shira's blog, and left this anonymous comment:

> Hey, who's the girl I saw with Brian Quinn after last week's show?

She had no idea if the new girl had been at last week's show, but it was worth a try.

There was an e-mail from her father, "gently reminding" her yet again to get her Denman application done. And one from Sheryl, written the night before.

> Subject: Bernie, birthday, etc.
> Time: 11:53:08 -0500
> From: Sheryl Quinn <yankfan472380@yahoo.com>
> To: Carly Finnegan <cfinnega@jbsg.org>
>
> Carly, honey—
> I got your message, and that was sweet of you to call. To think of me. Actually, it was my birthday, which made it even nicer that you were thinking of me. And I would have *loved* to see Bernie! And if I'd been in town, I would have hopped on a train and come right up. But we had people over, and it just wasn't a good time.
> I'm sorry to have to say this, but I think maybe for now at least it would be better for you if you didn't call

here. Brian told me he was going to tell you about the situation, and I know how much you must be hurting.

It's been a long time, but I've BEEN where you are! I do know how you feel. I know how hard it can be to let go.

Carly, you're a GREAT girl with a lot going for you. The best thing you can do for yourself is try to put your mind elsewhere.

So take care of yourself, okay? Maybe after some time goes by we can reconnect, but I really think this is for the best right now.

xxoo,

your friend,

Sheryl

It was a nice idea, putting her mind elsewhere. At the time, though, it was impossible.

There was nowhere else for her mind to go.

The next day she got the answer to her question from good old dependable ShiraZ.

ShiraZ

ERNESTINEISEVERYWHERE

You Heard It Here First: My Source tells me the new woman seen at Brian's side is Taylor Deen, photographer extraordinaire and senior at West Village Friends.

The pair got to know each other recently when Train hired Taylor to shoot a week of shows. My Source says he's "totally whacked" for her.

ShiraZ

Carly clicked on the <u>photographer extraordinaire</u> link, thinking she'd find flowers and sunsets or maybe some arty industrial landscapes. But instead she found herself face-to-face with Brian. Actually, all three of them: Brian and Liam and Avery, sitting backstage at Train all sweaty and smiling. She knew it was Train because she recognized the ratty couch. She'd sat on it enough times to know its stains and holes and cigarette burns intimately. Backstage at Train was quite the pit. But the black-and-white picture made it look cool and glamorous. The picture taker had perfectly captured that fired-up, we-killed-tonight glow the guys had after a good show.

Carly clicked through the whole series, which was aptly titled "Gig." It began with the guys unloading the van in the alley behind the club and then went through the whole show; sound check; guys onstage; crowded dance floor; the obligatory after-show mingle with fans cramped into Train's tiny greenroom; then equipment packing; van loading; and finally the empty, trash-strewn club at three a.m.

After she clicked through the whole series, she went back to get a better look at a shot of Brian onstage. This picture blew her away. It was the Brian she knew. The

Brian she thought *only* she knew. His eyes were closed, his head was bent slightly over the neck of his bass. She could tell that in his mind he was in that place he'd once described to her as "a warm red room where all that exists is rhythm."

She was about to click to the next picture when she glanced at the people crowded in front of the stage: the usual gaggle of girls staring up at Avery, practically salivating, and of course the skinny hipster wannabe boys with their eyes homed in on Avery's guitar. Some—the smart ones—studied Brian's bass. Then, off to the side of the crowd, she spied a familiar profile.

Her own.

She wasn't exactly skilled with photographic software, but she was highly motivated, and within minutes she managed to crop the shot and zoom in on herself.

It was not a pretty picture.

She had her arms crossed in front of her chest. Her face was mostly in shadow, but she could see the way her eyes were narrowed and her mouth scrunched up in a tight, ugly frown. She wasn't looking at Brian. She wasn't admiring or appreciating or adoring him. She was glaring at another girl who was admiring and appreciating and adoring him.

And this wasn't just any other girl. It was that girl she'd made the scene about, from Up All Night Records.

This was the night she'd made that scene.

The night Brian dumped her.

She clicked back to the after-show shots. She'd clicked through them quickly the first time, thinking they were generic crowd scenes. On closer inspection, she saw that they were focused on Liam and Avery and their groupies. In the first one, they were chatting up two smiley girls. But then off to the side, slightly out of focus, you could see Brian talking to the Up All Night girl. Diagonal to them, a few feet away, there she was, leaning against the wall and scowling in all her jealous ugliness.

In the next photo, two more girls had joined the Liam and Avery Admiration Society, and she'd gone from standing cross-armed and glaring to striding across the room, ready to claim her man from the would-be interloper.

Carly cringed as she clicked to the next picture. Liam and Avery were at the center. There were five girls now, three of them talking to Avery, the other two clearly settling for Liam while waiting to talk to Avery. But Brian was also in the frame. He was smiling, talking with his hands like he did when he was excited. The girl was smiling, too. From this angle Carly could see that it was an innocent, friendly conversation. The girl wasn't leaning in, breasts first, like those girls surrounding Liam and Avery. But out at the edge of the picture, there Carly was, making her way toward them, ready to bust it up.

She couldn't believe what she was seeing. The final seconds of her relationship caught on camera.

In the next one, Brian wasn't smiling anymore, and the girl looked surprised. Maybe even a little scared.

And who could blame her? Carly looked downright scary. The wrath of a woman scorned and all that. She'd positioned herself between them and had Brian by his resisting hand. Carly was smiling at the girl, a deranged don't-you-mess-with-my-man smile.

The next shot was a close-up on Liam and Avery's drama. They had their phones out and were taking numbers. The Up All Night girl was nowhere to be seen. Brian was talking to someone just outside the frame. He had both hands in his pockets, and his face had that awful look of annoyance Carly had seen just two days before when she'd done that stupid, desperate stop-by.

In the rest of the pictures Brian mostly had his back to the camera. But there was one that clearly showed his face. He was inside the van, sitting in the driver's seat, the door still open. Avery sat next to him in the passenger seat, checking his hair in the rearview mirror. Brian was looking directly into the camera, smiling.

The way he used to smile at her.

20

IN A matter of hours, after putting her considerable Bell-win School informational-literacy skills to work, Carly had filled several pages of a brand-new notebook with the highlights of Taylor Deen's charmed life.

She came from a well-known Greenwich Village family. The kind of family whose weddings and deaths and home remodelings got written up in the *New York Times*.

Her mother, Judith Monroe Deen, was the only child of Ben and Sadie Monroe, founders of the Monroe Gallery, "the epicenter of the sixties art scene." One article mentioned an unverified rumor that Sadie Monroe had been "romantically linked" with Bob Dylan before marrying Ben and that she was the Sadie mentioned in one of his more obscure songs. According to *Contemporary American Art* magazine, the Monroe Gallery was still considered "one of the art world's center rings." Getting a show there was considered "a clear indication of an artist's having 'arrived.'"

Ben and Sadie Monroe died tragically—together—

when their car ran off the road and tumbled into the sea in Jamaica, where they spent part of every winter at what their lengthy obituary called a "rustic island getaway." A thousand people, including Sir Paul McCartney and his then-wife, Linda (Stella's mother), who once showed her photographs at the gallery, attended the memorial service. Taylor's mother, who was only twenty-one at the time, inherited the gallery and the brownstone that held it, as well as the rustic island getaway.

Three years after her parents' obituary, Judith Monroe made the *Times* again for her wedding to R. Conrad "Duffy" Deen III, heir to the Deen furniture fortune and "independent scholar" of modernist art. This wasn't one of those three-paragraph jobs under a smiling studio portrait of the couple but a full-length article with details about how they met (at a dinner honoring an artist she was showing in the gallery), where they went for their first date (an experimental dance performance in Tribeca), and what the guests were served at the reception (poached salmon with a caviar cream sauce, just like at the dinner where the bride and groom first locked eyes across a crowded room).

A few years after the wedding, Judith and Duffy appeared in the Home section of the *Times*. They'd just done a major overhaul of the brownstone in anticipation of the birth of their first child. The smiling couple was pictured in the doorway of the nursery, each with a hand on Judith's swollen belly. The room looked nothing like the fluffy stuff you'd see in a Pottery Barn Kids catalogue. No baby animals. No fairies. No balloons. Instead they'd painted the walls deep red and hung abstract impressionist prints, which they thought would be "far more interesting to an infant's mind."

Carly checked the date and did the math. That lump was the future Taylor Deen.

True to her Village roots, and perhaps to that early exposure to fine art, Taylor grew into an artist herself. She'd been winning photography prizes, showing and publishing her pictures since she was ten. Her list of accomplishments included honorable mention in the Shoot Nations global youth photography contest and first prize in the *New York Times Magazine* contest for high-school students, as well as regional and national placement in the Scholastic Art & Writing competitions.

Once she ruled out the Up All Night girl, Carly had been half hoping that Brian's new "someone" would turn out to be one of those girls who were always trying to get his attention online or hanging around gigs slipping the guys their phone numbers and inviting them to parties.

If Brian had hooked up with a status-seeking groupie, Carly would know that he was just passing the time. It wouldn't last. He'd get bored. Not that she thought he was going to come back to her. She didn't. She just wanted to have mattered to him. She wanted what they'd had to mean as much to him as it did to her. If he were with one of those girls, Carly would be okay with it because she'd know that what she'd had with Brian was so much better. So much more real.

But this wasn't a girl looking for status. She didn't need it. She had plenty of her own.

Carly's image search yielded plenty of pictures *by* Taylor Deen, but only two measly pictures *of* Taylor Deen. One was taken when she was twelve, at an awards ceremony. Carly could see she was pretty, but she was a young-looking twelve, skinny and gangly. There was a more recent one on her school's Web site, but it was a group shot of kids who'd gone on a service trip to fix houses in New Orleans. Taylor was on the side, half in shadow, eyes half closed, talking to someone off camera.

There was no way Carly could friend her, so she couldn't get past the worthless thumbnail that showed only one eye and half a nose. If she wanted to see Taylor, it was going to have to be live and in person.

All she wanted was a glimpse. A face to go with the name. And so the following Saturday morning she took off to stake out the Deen family's brownstone until she got it.

PART
three

Nine Days Later

21

A person is guilty of stalking in the fourth degree
when he or she intentionally, and for no legitimate
purpose, engages in a course of conduct directed at a
specific person, and knows or reasonably should know
that such conduct:

1. is likely to cause reasonable fear of material harm
to the physical health, safety or property of such person, a member of such person's immediate family or a
third party with whom such person is acquainted. . . .

—New York State Criminal Code New York Penal
Law Section 120.45

THE PROSECUTOR, a friend of a friend of Taylor's family,
was threatening to charge Carly with stalking in the fourth
degree, a class B misdemeanor in the New York State criminal code, punishable by a $500 fine, three months in jail,
and/or a year's probation.

"*And*/or?" Carly's mother asked. "Are you sure it isn't
either/or?"

"Yes," Carly's lawyer said. "I don't think anyone's ever
gotten all three. And I've only heard of one or two cases

where someone actually did time, but theoretically, yes. If she's charged, she could have to pay a fine, do time, *and* have her whereabouts monitored by the state for a year after that. And the family wants an order of protection."

"A what?" asked Isabelle.

"A restraining order."

Carly studied the blonde woman in the dark blue suit sitting across the shiny, dark wooden table. *Her* lawyer. A lawyer of her very own. Of all the things she'd ever lain awake wishing she had, a lawyer wasn't one of them. But now she was very glad to have one.

Susan G. Whitman, Esq., was a friend of a friend of Nick's, a criminal-defense attorney who had agreed to meet with Carly, her mother, Nick, and—fresh off an early-morning flight from Ohio—Carly's father, Professor Tim Finnegan. The last time they'd all been in the same room— for the Bellwin School ceremony marking the end of eighth grade—the mood had been a bit more celebratory.

No, Susan explained, it didn't matter that Carly never intended to cause her specific person any fear.

"Intention has nothing to do with it. All that matters is whether what you did would cause a reasonable person to be concerned about their safety. And what you did . . ."

"I know, I know," Carly said. She placed her elbow on the table, cradled her forehead in her hand, and closed her eyes, wishing she could disappear. Or turn back time. Or wake up.

She wouldn't care if she woke up in that awful triangle with the flimsy curtain in the crappy sublet. Or on the hard futon in the guest room/office/storage room at her father's. Anywhere but the hushed conference room of Babcock & Whitman, Attorneys-at-Law, Specialists in Criminal Defense.

But the room was no figment of Carly's imagination.

It was clean. The walls, painted a soft yellow, displayed cheerful photographs of the great outdoors: snow-capped mountains, fields of blooming wildflowers, a seascape with a cavorting whale. The table looked freshly polished, and the cushioned chairs were as nice as the ones in her mother's office. Yet there was something in the air of this room. Not exactly a smell. A heaviness. Something she could almost taste. She imagined it to be the collected desperation of all the accused who'd ever sat around the big table.

Carly couldn't bring herself to look at her sighing mother or her bewildered, sleep-deprived father or Nick, who kept trying to catch her eye.

She lifted her head and, looking only at Susan G. Whitman, Esq., said, "I know what I did."

"But stalking? Why stalking?" Nick asked. "I thought this was about trespassing. That's what the police said—"

"Doesn't there have to be a pattern for stalking?" asked Isabelle. "A threat of some kind?"

"Why would she want to stalk this girl? Who is she?" her father wanted to know.

Carly kept her head down, but she could feel them all looking at her, waiting for her explanation.

Susan broke the silence. "Carly?"

Carly studied the wood grain in the table. Now that she looked closely, she could see it wasn't solid wood but veneer. Some of it had chipped away at the edge, revealing particleboard underneath.

"Carly," Susan said once more as she reached out and touched Carly's upper arm. "I know this is hard. But if I'm going to help you—and I think I can help you—you're going to have to help me."

She stopped and waited. Outside the closed door, phones rang and rang. Carly wondered what the people on the other end of those calls had done that needed the services of Babcock & Whitman.

Susan pushed the manila folder that had been sitting in front of her into the center of the table and opened it to a faint black-and-white picture from a printer in need of toner. Without lifting her head, Carly studied the picture.

At first all she saw was trees. There was no color, but the shades of gray and the partly empty branches told her it was fall. And then, through an opening in the trees, a bench.

She recognized the hat. Even in black and white it was still ugly and still too big for her. You couldn't see her face, because she was looking down, at her lap, at her Harriet the Spy notebook.

"What's that?" Carly's mother asked, peering into the center of the table.

Susan tried to get a response. "Carly?"

Now it was no longer a matter of refusing to speak. Carly couldn't speak. Her heart was pounding, and a strong tingling sensation ran through her whole body. She wondered if this was what a person felt like before fainting. She hoped so. She would have liked nothing more than to black out right then.

But Carly never was the fainting type.

Her mother reached for the picture and lifted it to her eyes, so she didn't see what the rest of them saw. Another picture beneath it. Same bench, same girl on the bench, but from a different angle. And close-up. Though she wasn't facing the camera directly, Carly's face was fully visible. She was looking at something. What? Oh, the swinging baby and her distracted, newspaper-reading father.

It was only a blur. If you didn't know you might think it was a bird, or a spot on the camera lens—but Carly knew, as the photographer had, too, that it was a little red shoe caught just after it slipped from the baby's foot. Which meant it was right before Taylor swooped in to retrieve it for the pervy father, saving him whatever grief his wife would dispense if he came home with a one-shoed baby.

Carly's father reached for that picture and held it to his eyes. There was another beneath it. "Who took these?"

"Taylor Deen took these pictures, Mr. Finnegan."

"The girl who—?"

"Yes."

Carly herself reached for the next picture, of the firemen showing off for Taylor. She remembered the look on the guy's face when Taylor burned him with the fake phone number and wished she could tell Nick the story. He would have loved that one.

But the firemen were beside the point. The reason this picture was in this folder was in the upper left corner. There she was again.

She thought back to that moment in the park. She'd had no idea what to do with herself when Taylor stopped to take pictures of the firemen. And so she'd stood there just kind of staring until she remembered to look busy. Just after that picture was snapped, she'd gotten out her phone and made the first of the many fake calls she'd make that day.

Carly's mother asked, "How many of these are there?"

Susan laid the rest out on the table.

In a shot of a crowded fish market in Chinatown, there was a close-up of Carly gazing into a tank of live fish and turtles. There she was again, surveying the mystery vegetables at Mean Vegetable Lady's store. There she was, placing stalks of bok choy in her brown bag.

Passing by a bodega later in the day. The ugly hat replaced by the trucker cap, the turquoise reading glasses replaced by the Paris Hilton sunglasses.

"Wait. Wait," Isabelle said. "This is someone else. Carly doesn't have a hat like that."

"Carly?" All four looked at her.

Her mouth and throat were dry, but she managed to croak out. "It's me. I bought the hat in Chinatown."

The last picture was a close-up of the bok-choy bomb that had ended Carly's adventure in spying.

"I don't know why that one's in here." Susan shrugged.

Carly didn't know, either, but she found the picture fascinating. The bok choy was strangely beautiful with its dark leaves splayed out against the grainy sidewalk, surrounded by dark circles of ancient spat-out gum and a lone, lipstick-stained cigarette butt. It was like Taylor had taken Carly's craziness and made it into art.

"Eight so far. The girl says she thinks there may be more. She hasn't looked at all of them from that day."

"But"—Carly's father shook his head as he spoke—"it looks to me like Carly is the one being stalked here."

"Yeah," said her mother, happy for a straw to grasp onto. "All I see here are pictures of my daughter walking around Manhattan, minding her own business, and somebody keeps taking pictures of her."

Her father reached for the one of her in the fish market. "How is this inducing fear in anyone?"

The room went quiet again while everyone stared at the pictures, then at Carly, then back to the pictures.

Finally Susan broke the silence. "Carly? Is that what's

going on here? Are you following or being followed?"

Carly didn't answer. Didn't even acknowledge the question. She was still looking at the bok choy.

"Carly." Susan was losing patience. "Your parents are suggesting that maybe you were the wronged party here. Is that the case?"

She closed her eyes, took a deep breath in through her nose, and said, "No."

Susan explained that these were parts of larger photographs that had been zoomed and cropped to show Carly. "Apparently, after what happened Friday, she and the boyfriend noticed Carly's presence in this series, all taken on one day last week."

"But I never meant to—I wasn't planning on . . ." Carly tried to explain how she'd never planned on following Taylor for the whole day. "I wasn't planning to follow her at all. I just wanted to know what she looked like. I thought it would help me."

For the first time that morning Carly looked directly at her mother. Expecting anger and annoyance, she was surprised to see teary eyes and trembling lips.

"I thought if I faced it, I'd get over it. If I saw her in the flesh, it would help me to finally move on."

"Then why follow her all day," Susan asked, "if all you wanted was a glimpse?"

"I don't know. I guess because I found her interesting. I wanted to know what she was like. I didn't want her to see me. I didn't want to hurt her. I kind of wished we could be friends."

"Let me stop you right there," said Susan. "What you just said, about liking her and wishing you could be friends?"

"Yeah?"

"That stays in this room, okay?" She pointed at Carly and repeated, "Okay?"

Carly nodded. "Okay. I didn't mean I thought we *could* be friends. I wasn't going to try to make her my friend. I just thought that if we knew each other some other way, then maybe we'd be friends."

"Got it. End of subject. Don't repeat that. Any of you." She went around the table with her index finger and stern look until she'd gotten a nod from Carly's mother, Carly's father, and Nick. "Not to the judge, not to the social worker when she interviews you. And this is probably the most important thing: not to their lawyer. Later, after we've gotten you diverted to treatment, and you have your own shrink and you have doctor-client privilege, then you can talk all you want about how you—'just wanted to be friends.' But—"

Carly's father broke in. "Hey—is that really necessary?"

"Is what necessary, Mr. Finnegan?"

"The whole tough-talking New York lawyer act."

Susan brought out the pointer finger again. "Is that what you think this is? An act?"

"Come on," said Carly's father, looking across the table

to his ex-wife. "Our daughter needs help. You said it your-self. I don't think it helps for you to be making fun of her."

Susan shot Nick an *is-he-for-real?* look and then turned to Carly's father.

"Okay, let's get something straight here. This is serious. Your daughter could end up with a criminal record. It's unlikely, but she could even see a few months in Rikers."

Carly's mother gasped. Susan put her hand on Carly's shoulder and squeezed. "That's not going to happen. I just need you and your parents to understand this is seri-ous. There's some pretty damning evidence against you, and these are some well-connected people you've messed with, and it's still an open question whether I can get you diverted into treatment. So I need you to be a big girl and help me understand what happened, okay?"

Carly just nodded this time. If she opened her mouth, she'd start crying, and she wasn't sure she'd be able to stop.

Susan kept her eyes on Carly and spoke calmly. "If the judge hears you say anything about wanting to be friends with Taylor, he might decide he needs to keep a closer eye on you. People have gotten hurt—killed, even—by de-ranged people who wanted to be their friends."

Judge. Social worker. Diverted to treatment. Carly couldn't believe she was hearing these words spoken about her. She lowered her eyes and tried to lose herself tracing the wood grain.

"Carly!" Nick yelled.

She looked up. Nick never yelled. "Stay with us. We need to know that you understand what Susan is saying here." She hadn't seen a look like that on Nick's face since he caught Jess fooling around with his blowtorch. He was seriously worried.

"I understand."

"Good, because you've got more explaining to do, young lady." Susan reached for the briefcase she'd placed on an empty chair next to her. She pulled out a single sheet of paper and put it in Carly's father's hands.

"What's this?"

"Read it," she said. "They just handed it to me. I only have the one copy. But it's out there on the Internet for anyone to see." Isabelle and Nick moved their chairs closer to Tim's, where they could read along.

Carly saw the banner at the top of the page and recognized the font.

ShiraZ
LITTLE MISS PSYCHO FAN

SECURITY BREACH! If you were at last night's EiE show, you might have noticed Bittersweet's two big bouncers running around, looking all serious, talking into their walkie-talkies like Secret Service guys on the trail of a would-be assassin. That's 'cause someone—

and I have reason to believe it's one of you, dear readers—told a big fat lie in order to gain free entry to the show under false pretenses.

Some teenage female personage, dressed like the Unabomber, claimed to be the girlfriend of a band member. A girlfriend whose name was revealed one week ago in this very blog!

Now, now, Ernestine fans. Devotion is a good thing. The word "fan," after all, is short for "fanatic." Without our devotion and enthusiasm, who knows if the guys would have just SIGNED WITH A MAJOR RECORDING LABEL (yes!). But this is taking your devotion too far.

It's one thing to dream about someday being the girlfriend of a member of what I think we can all agree is New York's hottest band. I myself have dreamed such dreams. But honeys, it's quite another to cut to the front of the line and say you're someone you're not.

Okay, Imposter Girl, listen up: Maybe you think it's funny. Maybe you were broke and couldn't afford the cover. I hope it's something like that. I hope it's not that in some twisted way you think you're Brian's destiny or something, because—well, because that would be nuts, and you would seriously need some serious professional help.

(I'm sorry to go on like this when most of you dear readers are innocent bystanders who might not, until now, have even been aware of the situation. But since it's been pointed out to me by people who matter that it's very likely that the perpetrator of this crime got the information she used right here, I cannot keep silent.)

You have undermined the trust this blogger has worked so hard to earn with Ernestine is Everywhere band members and management. Your little prank could cost the rest of us SANE fans access to the information we need to support our not-so-struggling-anymore musicians.

Yo, Little Miss Psycho Fan: Get a life!!

Shira

"Their lawyer is saying this is more evidence of your obsession with his client. A desire to be her. And possibly to do her harm."

Carly watched the blood drain from her mother's face as she read about what happened at Bittersweet. When she got to the bottom of the page, Isabelle looked at her and in a voice barely above a whisper said, "That's you? Little Miss Psycho Fan?"

Carly nodded. "But it's not what it sounds like. I didn't want to be her. I was only doing it so I didn't have to wait on line. It was cold."

"What night was this?" Carly's mother looked over her father's shoulder at the printout.

"Last Sunday," Carly said.

"And where was I?"

"You were asleep."

"Wait a second," her father said. "Didn't I talk to you that night?"

"Yeah."

"And you told me you were walking on Broadway, heading home from Val's."

"I was on Broadway, but I wasn't heading home."

Nick asked why she would be going to Brian's show if they were broken up.

"I was going to say good-bye." It sounded so stupid now. So obviously an excuse. But at the time, she'd believed her own excuses. Maybe it was sleep deprivation—she had hardly slept the night after the day she'd spent following Taylor—but she really had convinced herself that going to Brian's show and saying a silent good-bye would help her put an end to the obsession that was starting to get seriously out of hand.

"So he was expecting you?" Susan sounded skeptical.

"No. I wasn't going to say good-bye to his face. I was doing it for myself. I realized that following Taylor around like that wasn't right. I knew I needed to stop. And so when I read that they were going out on tour after their show Sunday night, I decided to go. I was making a ritual out of it, like Val and I sometimes do."

"Did Val know about this?" Isabelle asked.

"No."

Carly wondered what—if anything—Val knew about what she'd done. On Susan's recommendation, they'd taken everything away from her: her phone, her laptop. And Isabelle was watching her like a hawk at the apartment.

22

THE LITTLE Miss Psycho event happened on the Sunday after she'd followed Taylor.

After spending the night at Val's, Carly headed downtown to pick Jess up at Nick's. The two of them returned to the sublet to find a jar of spaghetti sauce and a note asking Carly to make dinner and see that Jess got to bed with a uniform ready for the morning. Isabelle had a headache.

Isabelle's migraine medication always put her into a deep slumber. When it was time for Jess to go to sleep, they found her sprawled out across the bed with a sleeping mask over her eyes, slack jawed, drooling, and snoring up a pharmaceutically induced storm.

Jess stood by the side of the bed, arms folded in front of her. "Can't I sleep in your room?"

"What room? I don't have a room; I have a bed. And no, you can't. I have homework. I'll have the light on for hours."

"I'll use this," she said, starting to slide the eye mask off Isabelle's face.

Carly reached out to stop her. "No."

"Why not? She never wakes up when she's like this."

"I know. That's why we're going to move her. If we roll her onto her side, she'll stop snoring, and there'll be enough room for you."

"Great," Jess said. "Where's my raincoat?"

"Oh, come on, it's not that bad. Like you never drool?"

Carly pulled the covers off. Isabelle was in her underwear: a frayed deep purple bra and black bikini panties, a combination that might have been sexy once, but now, in combination with her mismatched socks—one white, one blue—only looked sad to Carly. She hadn't seen her mother undressed for a while and was surprised to see how thin she'd gotten, how tightly her flesh was stretched over her bones. She was warm and slightly damp with sweat.

"Okay," Carly whispered, though it would take a lot more than talking to rouse her mother. "Grab her feet on 'three.' One, two, three."

Jess reached across the bed and pulled the sprawled-out foot back to join the other, while Carly did the same with the sprawled-out arm. Jess held the feet and hands down while Carly walked around the bed, climbed in behind her mother, and pushed from behind. With a groaning, mumbling sigh, she rolled onto her side, curled into fetal position, and yawned.

"That's it, Isabelle," Carly said, stroking her damp hair. "Breathe your stress away."

After another deep yawn, Isabelle's breathing settled

into a rhythm and Jess crawled in the other side.

Carly turned on the noise machine to Jess's choice of crashing waves. "Remember, if she rolls back and starts again, you just push from the shoulders."

"Okayyy," Jess said, her voice full of complaint. "But if she smushes me and I can't get her back over, I'm coming into your bed."

Carly bent down and kissed her sister's forehead. "Sure." But Jess was a sound sleeper. Carly knew she wouldn't wake up once she was asleep.

As she sat down at her computer, Carly fully intended to work on her admissions essay for Denman. But after five minutes, she was on the Ernestine is Everywhere Web site. They had a show that night. Uptown. Not too far from the sublet. It was going to be their last New York show before leaving on tour.

Sitting in the law offices of Babcock & Whitman, looking at Shira's printed-out blog entry, she tried to capture the frame of mind in which she had showered, dressed in black, and slicked down her hair. Her reasons were murky, even to herself. She had a half-baked, half-assed idea about facing the truth and accepting it. Of needing to see the truth in order to accept it. But that didn't explain what she did when she got there. It was, as Shira said, totally psycho.

Her father sat up in his chair, placed his hands on the table, and leaned over. "But you gave that girl's name at the door?" Carly saw a look pass between her parents. It reminded her of how Jolie Albright's parents looked when they talked about their daughter.

Surely she wasn't that far gone, was she? This could still come out okay, couldn't it? "When I got there—the line was so long. I just—I wasn't thinking it through. I just wanted to get out of the cold. And there were so many people, it looked like they would be turning some away, and so—I knew her name would be on the list because they always put the girlfriends on, even if they're not coming to the show. It was a school night. I didn't think she'd be there, so I said I was her just so I could get in."

The truth was, she didn't know why she did what she did. At the time, she told herself it was just to get in the door. She'd never had to wait in line for an Ernestine show. She'd never had to pay a cover and never had to show ID. She always either arrived with the band—or else the bouncers, like at Train, already knew her.

When she got to Bittersweet that night and saw the line, she walked all the way to the end of the block and actually stood in line for a while. But no one moved. If she hadn't done what she'd done, she wouldn't have gotten in. At that point, she was too far gone to see that not getting in wasn't a bad thing.

So she made her way to the front, passing clumps of people she recognized from Ernestine shows at Train.

Shira Zeidman was there, surrounded by a group of kids from Performing Arts. She was smoking a cigarette and texting furiously. Carly pulled her hood up and forward to hide her face, then kept her eyes on the sidewalk as she passed.

She tried to act casual as she approached the two big, stony-faced, crossed-armed bouncers.

"Hi. I'm supposed to be on the list? Taylor Deen? I'm Brian Quinn's girlfriend."

The guy looked her in the eye and held her gaze. She could feel herself reddening. Did he know the real Taylor Deen? Was she already there?

He picked up the clipboard sitting on the stool next to him and skimmed the list.

"He's the bass player. . . ."

The guy nodded. "Taylor Deen, Taylor Deen. I'm not seeing— Wait, wait. Yup. Here you are, Taylor Deen." He put the clipboard back and actually smiled at her. "Got some ID?"

"What?"

"I said ID, sugar. Got some ID? I gotta ask everyone. Even girlfriends." The smile faded and the stony face reappeared.

She wasn't prepared for this. She'd never been asked for ID when she was with the band.

"Oh, I don't want to drink. You can just give me one of the green bracelets."

"Yeah," he said, like he'd said it a hundred times before. "See, we need proof. Eighteen and up means no one under eighteen gets in. It's not just about who can drink and who can't."

"I'm eighteen, I swear. My birthday was in September. The seventeenth." This was Taylor's actual birthday.

He nodded, crossed his arms.

She smiled. Confident and friendly, as she imagined Taylor would smile. "What's your name?"

"Finn."

"Hi, Finn," she said, and turned to the other one, who was holding a flashlight up to some kid's driver's license. The bouncer didn't answer, and she couldn't tell if it was because he didn't hear her or just didn't want to hear her.

"That's Mike," Finn said. "He doesn't talk much."

"Well, Finn." Again she smiled. "Do you think you could let me slide this time? I'm Brian's . . . girlfriend. The bass player?"

Finn looked at his watch, then over her shoulder at the line of eager Ernestine fans behind her.

"It was really stupid of me, I know. See, I was supposed to meet up with them earlier, and come with them, but, well—it's a long story, and you don't need all the details. I just didn't think I'd need my ID. The guys at Train know me. And I never need it there, so . . ." She shrugged and held her hands out apologetically.

She didn't see the walkie-talkie until he brought it up

to his mouth and pushed the button. "Yo, John?"

He released the button and looked at her while he waited for a response. The walkie-talkie blipped, and a fuzzy voice said, "Yo." She did her best to look unfazed, not worried in the least, while her heart pounded.

Finn brought it back to his mouth, pushed the button and said, "Yeah, I got a girl out here. Taylor Deen. She's on the list. A girlfriend. No ID." He released the button. Waited.

Blip. Fuzz. "Yeah, what'd you say the name was?"

Finn held the walkie-talkie closer to his mouth. "Taylor. Deen."

Carly hoped nobody within hearing range knew Taylor.

Blip. Fuzz. "Hold on, I'll check."

"Okay."

She stood there, frozen, imagining Brian backstage, running scales, practicing riffs, doing those finger stretches he always did before playing. What if he came out to help?

She'd run. She'd head up Broadway, as fast as she could.

Blip. Fuzz.

Finn brought the walkie-talkie up to his ear and looked straight at her while listening to the verdict. "It's cool. Let her in."

The bracelet guy slapped a bright green one on her wrist. "You want someone to take you backstage?" Finn asked. "It says here"—he pointed to the typed guest list, on the clipboard—"you're 'All Access.'"

"Oh, no, that's okay. Maybe later. I don't want to get in the way back there. Thanks so much for helping me. And for understanding about the ID. I really appreciate that."

"No problem. Next time you better have it, though."

"Oh, I will, don't worry."

She walked into the dark, crowded club. The opening band was still playing. Their vocalist, a tiny, pasty-faced girl with bleached-blonde hair and a strangely deep voice, was strutting and stomping with what appeared to be all her might. They weren't bad. But hardly anyone except a small group in front of the stage paid them any attention.

It was an Ernestine crowd.

Carly got in line to buy a Coke and wound up behind a group of Columbia students trading Ernestine stories. When and how they first heard them. What shows they'd been to, how they thought the record deal was going to affect the music.

Someone started bragging—loudly—about how he knew them before anyone heard of them.

"Yeah?"

"Yeah, I worked with them last summer, upstate."

Carly looked for the source of the voice, and there was Cameron Foster, still wearing his puka beads and smiling his charming smile.

"Really? Wow." A dreamy girl looked up at Cameron. "Doing what?"

"We worked at this camp together. They're really cool."

"That's amazing, Cameron," Dreamy (and possibly Stoned) Girl said. "Are they, like, as cool as they seem? Because they seem totally cool."

"Yeah, they were really mellow and"—he paused to find the right word—"unassuming."

Hah. *Unassuming*. What a joke.

Carly kept her head down, bought her Coke, and climbed up to the second-floor loft, where she found an empty stool in a dark corner, next to a half wall overlooking the stage. The opening act finished their last song, and their friends up front went nuts. Most people kept on talking.

The two guys next to her were deep in philosophical conversation.

"So we get to her room, and things start to get hot. She's all over me. It's nuts. It's like she can't get my clothes off fast enough."

"You liar."

"I swear, but wait, you have to hear what happens next. So we're all over each other. Clothes are flying this way and that. She's asking me if I have a condom."

"And you're making this up."

"Dude. I'm not—would you just listen?"

"Okay. Okay. She's all over you, begging for it."

"Practically, yeah. I mean, I'm not exactly trying to fight her off or anything."

"Right. And then?"

"And then her roommate walks in."

"Yeah?"

"And she looks at us."

"Yeah?"

"And she doesn't say anything. She doesn't turn around and leave, doesn't ask us to leave. Doesn't. Say. Anything. Ashley, the girl I'm with, says 'Hey, Heather.' And Heather says 'Hey, Ashley.' And then she sits down at her desk and opens her laptop."

"Yeah?"

"And so I'm reaching for my shirt and trying to zip up my pants, and Ashley goes, 'What are you doing?' and I say, 'I'm leaving.' And she says, 'Why?' And I say, 'Um, 'cause your roommate just walked in?' And she says, 'That's okay. She doesn't care.'"

"Dude! No. And so what did you do?"

"I got my shit and got the hell out of there."

"No."

"What was I supposed to do, keep going while the roommate was sitting there? For all I know, the two of them had a camera going and were streaming it live."

"Wouldn't stop me."

"Dude, you're sick."

"Dude, you're the sick one. Why doesn't this stuff ever happen to me? I'd be down with it. Roommate wants to watch? Fine. Maybe she'd like to join us. Anyone else? Come on in."

Carly knew that conversations like that took place all the time. And not just between guys, either. She'd heard girls at school say worse. Still, it was creepy to be standing practically in the middle of this one, unable to move without losing her view of the stage.

Brian never talked about girls that way. And if Liam or Avery or some guy started that kind of talk he'd find a way to change the subject or suddenly remember something he'd left in the van or a call he had to make. He never got all self-righteous about it; he just didn't go along with that bragging tell-all stuff.

"Now, that's sick," the storyteller said to the listener.

"No. It's just practical. A man has to take these opportunities when they come along."

There was no response to this pronouncement because right then, the house lights went down and the stage lights went up. Conversations dropped off and people started cheering as Liam and Avery strode onstage, looking out into the crowd., Brian walked out last, keeping his head down.

To someone who didn't know him, he might appear shy. But Carly knew the lowered head meant he was focusing, gathering his energy.

As soon as Liam sat, and Brian and Avery strapped on their guitars, they launched into "Mailman," and the audience was on its feet. Some sang along. Brian's eyes were closed, his head moving slightly to the beat.

She wondered if the sound guy had them mixed right, because it seemed like *all* she could hear was Brian's bass. She could feel it, too, traveling through her body. She watched his fingers move along the frets and curve around the strings and remembered how those fingers used to stroke her neck and slide down her spine before coming to rest in the small of her back.

For a second, she indulged the memory. She closed her eyes and imagined Brian standing behind her. All she'd have to do was lean back and his arms would circle her waist, his lips would find that place on her neck.

She snapped out of the reverie when she almost fell off the stool.

She tried to focus on her reason for being there. She was saying good-bye. She was putting the past behind her and moving forward with her life.

She tried to focus on being happy for Brian. He'd worked so hard, and now he was finally getting recognition. She looked around the club. It was twice as big as Train, and it was packed. She'd never seen them in front of a crowd that big. People were still coming in, too. Finn and Mike were still at the door, checking a steady flow of IDs.

"Mailman" ended to long, loud applause. Avery took off the Strat, put it on a stand behind him, and picked up his beloved Gibson acoustic while the clapping died down. Brian stayed in his corner, smiling at no one in particular.

When Avery got back to the mic, there was more applause.

"Thank you. Thank you very much." He waited for the second wave of applause to die out and said, "So this next one is our newest. My brother here—" He held his arm out toward Brian, who nodded shyly while people applauded and hooted and whistled. "My brother Brian here writes all our songs. Don't ask me where he gets his ideas. Although with this one I think maybe I know. See, there's this girl—"

Carly's stomach tightened. Her throat contracted.

Everyone else laughed.

"Oh, wow. This is so bizarre. There she is—" Avery held an arm out toward the door and every head in the house turned to see Taylor laughing as she talked to Finn and Mike, whose stony faces seemed to light up in her presence. She shook her head, pulled an ID out of the back pocket of her jeans, and handed it to Finn, who handed it to Mike, who shined his flashlight on it. She kept talking, seemingly oblivious to the fact that everyone in the entire club was looking at her.

Carly had to get out of there. Fast.

She'd seen an EXIT sign on her way upstairs. It was

over the door to the hall where the bathrooms were. She could be down the stairs and out back before they even started looking for her. But she couldn't pull herself away. She needed to see what happened next.

"Hey, Taylor." Avery had one hand over his eyes to block out the glare of the lights. He gave a little wave with the other and Taylor finally turned around and looked up on the stage, surprised. "Oh, hey, Ma." Everyone laughed again and looked back at the door. Sure enough, there was Sheryl, standing right behind Taylor, talking excitedly to Finn while digging through her purse. When she pulled out a wallet, she held it up in the air like a trophy.

"Hey, Mr. Doorman, that's my moms. You gots to let her in."

More laughter. Sheryl was laughing, too, gesturing toward the stage and nodding. Even Finn was laughing.

"Anyway," Avery continued his introduction, "the name of this song is, 'Same Goes for Me.'" He turned toward Brian, who counted off.

Carly looked back at the door. Sheryl and Taylor were gone, and Finn wasn't smiling anymore.

He was scanning the crowd, looking for the fake girlfriend.

The imposter.

The wannabe.

The usta-be.

She started moving. The place was a lot more crowded

now, and she had to squeeze her way through a lot of bodies.

"Excuse me. Sorry. Excuse me."

She'd seen Shira Zeidman in the crowd and steered clear of her. Not that she thought Shira even knew who she was, but just in case.

Some people stepped aside or leaned back to give her space. Others gave her dirty looks and refused to budge. Eventually she made it to the bottom of the stairs. She peeked around the corner to the door. Taylor was nowhere in sight. Finn and Mike were huddled with another grim-faced, official-looking guy. Finn handed that guy the clipboard and took off toward the front of the club, walkie-talkie in hand, scanning the crowd. Mike went the other way, also holding a walkie-talkie.

She followed the EXIT sign down to the end of the hall where the bathrooms were. The exit was a big, heavy door with a red handle that read:

CAUTION. FOR EMERGENCY USE ONLY.
Opening this door will cause an alarm to sound.

Carly ran through her options in her head: She could open the door, trigger the alarm, and run for it. How far would she get before Finn and Mike picked up the trail? What did she even know about what was behind the door? What if she couldn't find her way out of the alley?

Catty-corner to the exit was one more door, marked
EMPLOYEES ONLY. It was open slightly. She peeked in to
see a long, dimly lit staircase and cases of beer stacked
along the wall at the bottom. She considered heading
down, hiding in the basement until closing, and then mixing into the crowd when everyone left. She could ditch the
hoodie, let her hair down.

Before she could think this plan through, she heard the
blip and fuzz of a walkie-talkie and saw someone heading
up the stairs from the basement.

The voice on the walkie-talkie asked, "You check the
basement?"

As the footsteps got closer, she heard her friend Finn
say, "Yup."

She held her breath, pushed the emergency handle,
and braced herself for the alarm. The door gave without
a sound, opening onto an alley that smelled of cigarette
smoke mixed with garbage mixed with something buttery
and sweet.

A guy in a stained white jacket and checked pants stood
outside the kitchen of the restaurant next door, smoking a
cigarette and speaking Spanish into a cell phone. Behind
him she heard the clatter and bang of pots and pans and
happy, accordion-heavy music.

He kept talking on his phone as he looked Carly up
and down.

"Hi," she said, smiling, trying not to look scared or

guilty despite feeling very much of both. "Um, *hola*. Excuse me. *Por favor*. Can you tell me which way is out?"

Bittersweet was about a third of the way down a long block. From where she stood, the shorter way to the end of the block looked dark, like maybe it was a dead end, like maybe she didn't want to walk down it alone. It would take longer to get to the other, well-lit end, but it was a much less scary prospect.

He shrugged, took another drag off his cigarette and said *"Nada"* into the phone.

For a girl with a Puerto Rican best friend and a job in that best friend's family's restaurant, Carly had a pathetic command of Spanish. But she tried. *"Dónde es la—la—"* She had no idea how to say *out* or *exit*, so she said *"puerta,"* door.

He stared at her and pointed to the door she just came out of, then turned his back, like he didn't want anything to do with the crazy *chica* yelling at him in the alley.

"No. No. Out of *here*." He turned back around. She pointed down with both hands. And then up, to indicate over the building, toward the street. "How do I get out?!" She was practically shouting, in that obnoxious way people do when trying to communicate with someone who doesn't speak their language. But she didn't care how she looked, or sounded. She was desperate. Finn and Mike could burst through that exit any second.

Her desperation must have come through, because the guy ended his conversation with a quick "*Adiós*," closed his phone, and pointed down the alley toward the dark, short end.

"Or you can go through here," he said, nodding toward the kitchen.

His English was perfect, like he was born and raised in New York. Not even a trace of an accent. Carly should have felt like an idiot, but she was too busy feeling like a criminal. A criminal about to get caught.

"Some guy bothering you or something?"

"Something like that," she said as she stepped through the *puerta*.

Carly looked around the shiny wood table at her parents, her ex-almost stepfather, and her lawyer. "Really. It didn't have anything to do with wanting to be her. I just didn't want to wait on line."

Susan took a deep, skeptical breath and said, "Okay. Let's say we tell them that bit about you just wanting to get into the club to say a silent good-bye. How in the world do we explain what you did Friday night?"

Carly wished she knew.

23

AFTER THE Bittersweet incident, Carly thought for sure she was done with what she could see perfectly clearly was crazy behavior. Getting chased into a dark alley by two large men for having gained entry to a club under false pretenses will do that.

So she vowed to herself that it was the end.

Four days. She had four days of normalcy. She finished her paper on the Triangle Fire. Wrote her essay for Denman. It was pretty good, too. She wrote about that first trip to Turkey and how it hooked her on archaeology.

She was beginning to feel like she might be able to put it all behind her.

And then Friday rolled around.

Isabelle and her sister Nancy decided to go on a spa weekend, and Isabelle didn't want Carly staying alone in the apartment. Normally she would have stayed at Val's, but Val was visiting Cornell that weekend. Carly didn't want to spend the weekend at Nick's.

She hadn't recrossed the threshold between Nick's studio and the rest of the loft since leaving in June. She knew that even a glimpse of the river or the sight of sun pouring through the floor-to-ceiling windows onto the hardwood floors would make going back to the hovel even more torturous. The loft was home. But it was no longer hers.

And from what Jess had told her, it sounded like it was soon going to be Chantal's.

Nick had been urging Carly to come down and hang out ever since she got back from Stony Hollow. She still had a key. He told her she could come anytime, whether he was home or not. She could hang out, maybe do her homework. Whatever she wanted. When Isabelle made her plans for the spa weekend, he amped up his case. It would just be the three of them: Carly and Jess and him.

"We'll get a veggie special from Salvatore's. Rent a movie."

When Carly didn't jump at the invitation, Nick brought out the guilt.

"You know, Carly, I think this would be good for Jess. She told me she's worried about you. And with your mother's depression, I'm worried about her. She needs her big sister."

How could she refuse?

Carly was used to the strange feeling she'd get whenever she stepped off the train at Fourteenth Street now that it was no longer her station. But that Friday afternoon, with the prospect of a whole weekend at the loft ahead of her, it was worse. Her body felt like it was heading home, but her mind knew otherwise, and the confusion made her slightly dizzy.

They passed the newsstand where her mother used to buy the *Times* from Saleem in the morning and the *Post* from Raj in the afternoon, but the face looking out now was a stranger's. She'd never seen the man playing saxophone or the two transit cops who stood by the stairs, eyeing the crowd and talking about some Johnny Depp movie they both saw. Carly used to know all the buskers and cops, if not by name, then at least by sight. These people were strangers.

Even with Jess's hand in hers, she felt isolated and alone and cranky. As they headed from the subway stop to the loft, Carly found herself hating everyone she saw. Skinny women with blown-out hair clomping along on their skinny high heels. Overly groomed men in their casual designer clothes. Blinged-out gangsta wannabes.

And their little dogs, too. Everyone seemed to have a little dog in a little designer dog bag.

Black SUVs with tinted windows were double- and triple-parked along the street, their suited drivers out on the sidewalk, talking into cell phones or smoking cigarettes or checking out the women. Like the two tall, blonde ones bent over a map on the sidewalk ahead. They were arguing in a language Carly thought might be Swedish or maybe Norwegian, one of them jabbing the book with one finger, and pointing down the street with the other, saying, *"Ja! Ja!* Stella McCartney."

When they turned and started walking east, Carly thought it was funny. But Jess, smart, nice seven-year-old city girl that she was, ran after them to correct their mistake. Their destination, that holy shrine of fashion, was one block west.

Jess returned to her sister's side aglow with the satisfaction of her good deed.

"You know what your problem is, Jess? You're too nice."

"That is not a problem. You can't be too nice. That's like being too good or too smart."

"You might want to reconsider that position when you're a little older. I would have just let those two clomp all the way to the East River."

"Why?"

"'Cause I can't stand those people."

"You don't even know those people! You don't even know their *names*, Carly. How can you know you don't like them?"

"Oh, I know. Trust me. And someday you're going to, too."

"I hope not. I hope I'm not going to hate people I don't even know. Why are you in such a bad mood?"

"Me?"

"You should cheer up. It's going to be fun tonight. Like a sleepover. Only it isn't, because I live there—sort of—and you used to, and we're related."

"Yeah, so what is it?"

"I don't know. It's too complicated." Jess stayed quiet until they arrived at Nick's building. Then, as Carly put her key into the outside lock, Jess said, "I wish we still lived here."

"Tell me about it. At least you're here half the time."

When the lock buzzed, Jess pulled the door open. "I mean all of us. All the time. I don't like doing half and half. Sometimes I wake up in the morning and I don't know which bed I'm in. Then I keep my eyes closed on purpose and try to figure it out from the sounds. If Mom's snoring, or too close to me, it's easy."

"That's good. So you make a game out of it." Carly pushed the button for the elevator and leaned against the wall while it clanged its way down to the lobby.

"Yeah. I guess. It's not the funnest game, though."

The studio was empty. Nick had left a note saying he'd be back soon. Jess ran to her room to play on her computer while Carly took her first cautious steps into her former home.

Things looked pretty much the same in the big central room. Carly spent a few minutes staring out at the view before moving on to the kitchen.

At first she couldn't tell what was different. Then she noticed the shiny copper pots and pans hanging from a rack above the stove. A row of French cookbooks was lined up along the counter next to the stove. One of them, *La Cuisine Végétarienne*, lay faceup.

She wasn't planning to look in the room formerly known as her mother and Nick's, but the door was wide open. She not only looked, but took a few steps into the room. The king-sized bed had a new, expensive-looking comforter: deep ruby red, with a pattern of gold circles and squares woven in. On top of that was a small mountain of red and gold throw pillows. A half-empty pump bottle of lotion sat on the nightstand on what used to be her mother's side of the bed, along with a pile of books.

Despite these signs of change, nothing prepared her for what she found when she opened the door to her room.

Only the view was the same. The bed had been pushed back into a corner. A bunch of cardboard boxes—some open with rolls of paper sticking out, some sealed with packing tape—sat on top of the now-bare mattress. Several big plastic jugs, filled with what looked like paint, sat on the desk. Next to the desk, under the window where her bed used to be, was some kind of old-fashioned machine. It had wrought-iron legs and what looked like a steering wheel on one side. Next to the machine, lit by late-afternoon sun, was a long folding table covered with cards of assorted colors, arranged in a neat row. On each

card was the same poem, but each version was in a different font and different color ink. She picked one up just as
Nick walked into the room.

"Here you are. I'm sorry I was out. I was going to—"

"What is all this?"

"Chantal had to move out of her studio." Nick walked
over to Carly and put a hand on her shoulder. "It happened
pretty suddenly. They sold the building and offered everyone cash, and—"

"Oh," Carly said. Over Nick's shoulder she saw a flock
of geese heading upriver.

"I'm sorry. I should have warned you."

"Why?" She shrugged and pretended not to care. "It's
your place. I can't expect you to keep it like a museum.
'Carly Finnegan slept here.'" She took a step toward the
machine-thing. "You haven't answered my question. What
is this?"

"It's an antique letterpress." He picked up one of the
poems and held it up for her inspection. "You can simulate
this with computers, but it doesn't begin to compare to
the real thing. Each letter is done individually—and backward. Here, feel it."

Carly ran her finger over the words. "Tie Your Heart at
Night to Mine, Love." The thick paper felt rough against
her skin. Each letter formed its own indentation. "Mmm"
was all she could manage to get out.

"It's a dying art." Nick laid the poem down on the table and straightened the row. "This couple is driving Chantal crazy. It's for their wedding. They wanted to see the poem in every font she had, in every possible combination of ink and paper. It's incredibly labor-intensive. Each one of these letters is made with a lead slug, which she arranges by hand. Then she rolls each piece through one at a time."

"Uh-huh." Carly had nothing against Chantal, but she just couldn't join Nick in his indignation on her behalf. Was she living here? Or just working here? Where was she now? Was Chantal part of the pizza-and-sleepover plan?

"I meant to clear this off before you got here." He walked to the bed and picked up one of the boxes.

"It's okay, Nick. I'll sleep in Jess's room."

"No. No. We can clear this stuff off." He picked up another box and carried it to the corner where he'd started to stack them.

"Really. It's okay." It wasn't okay, but moving the boxes from the bed to the floor wasn't going to make it okay. Nothing she could think of—short of traveling back in time—was going to make anything okay. But she let Nick make himself feel better by clearing off the bed that wasn't hers anymore. She stood at the table in front of the window and watched a tour boat circle the lit-up Statue of Liberty.

A piece of paper from one of the boxes fell to the floor at her feet. She reached down to pick it up. She was barely looking at the thing, but two words leapt out: *Monroe* and *Gallery*.

It was a listing of November openings printed out from artdealers.org. Chantal—or someone—had circled a few of the others with a thick red marker, but not the one that caught Carly's eye.

Monroe Gallery
Esperanza Williams:
New Works
Opening Reception November 30th, 7:00 p.m.
This young Canadian painter's work has been called "haunting and disturbing," as well as "quirky and whimsical." These new paintings will defy those who insist on labels. Through February 10.

It was strange to think about, but if that piece of paper hadn't fallen at her feet at that moment, she probably wouldn't be sitting around the Babcock & Whitman, Attorneys-at-Law, Specialists in Criminal Defense table with four sets of eyes focused so intently on her.

A couple hours after the gallery listings fell at her feet, Carly found herself standing on the steps of the apartment building across the street from the Monroe Gallery. One large spot-lit painting hung in the gallery's window. In front of that, a small crowd milled around on the sidewalk, talking, smoking, and giving each other the once-over, trying to figure out who mattered, whose names would appear in write-ups of the event. Each time a cab (or in one case a Town Car) pulled up to the curb, all eyes would be on the passenger door, waiting to see who emerged.

She'd left the apartment saying she needed a little time to herself. She knew it was going to be hard going back to the loft. And she knew "her" room was never going to be hers anymore. But seeing it taken over like that was a lot harder than she'd anticipated. She assured Nick that she was fine. A brisk walk in the cold would do her good. Maybe she'd give Val a call. Things weren't exactly back to how they used to be between them. How could they be when Carly was hiding so much? But this topic was safe. Val knew how hard it had been to move away from Nick's, how upset she'd been when he and her mother broke up. Val would know what to say.

But Val's phone must have been off. Carly tried three times, and each time it went straight to voice mail.

So Carly walked. In the direction of the Monroe Gallery. She told herself she was just going to pass by. Maybe look in the windows and check out the art. See how big a crowd they got for their openings. For curiosity's sake.

- - -

But that's not what happened. Instead of passing by, she planted herself on the steps of a small apartment building across the street from the brownstone and gallery for a good five or ten minutes, staring up at the second-floor windows, where lights were going on and off and shadows were flitting across rooms. According to that *Times* piece she'd read, the Deen brownstone had six thousand square feet of living space in the four floors above the gallery. That would be a lot of space anywhere, but in New York City it was downright palatial. As far as Carly knew—and she knew pretty much everything in the public record—Taylor didn't have any siblings. So for each member of this family of three, there was the equivalent of a good-sized apartment's worth of square footage.

She wondered which of the windows were Taylor's. For some reason—maybe because it was thirty degrees out and she'd left without a hat or gloves—she pictured a huge room with a stone fireplace complete with roaring fire. Was Taylor in there now? Did that hand, pulling that curtain closed, belong to her?

A few people who lived in the building passed by on their way in or out. Most ignored Carly. Some gave her long, hard stares as they passed her on the steps. When an old woman pushing a shopping cart piled high with clanking bottles and cans down the sidewalk stopped to tell her, "They got free soup at Saint Mark's Church tonight," she decided she wouldn't ignore this obvious IM from the universe.

It was time to go.

The walk downtown and that little bit of harmless people-watching had calmed her down enough that she felt she could go back to Nick's and participate in the movie night Jess and Nick had planned without sulking. Sleeping in Jess's room wouldn't be so bad. Yes, it was pretty awful to see what had once been her space invaded by Chantal, but that room wouldn't have been hers forever. She'd have other rooms of her own. A dorm, next year, to start. And others after that.

That's how close Carly came to saving herself from all the trouble contained in that file folder.

She glanced across the street for one last look just as the front door of the main residence, one floor above the gallery, opened and Taylor walked out. She was with two friends. All three seemed to be talking at once as they traipsed down the stairs, linked arms, and headed up West Fourth Street.

Carly watched for a while, and she'd be lying if she said she didn't consider following Taylor again. She knew Brian was on the road. Probably up in Canada by now, according to the tour itinerary they'd posted. What would a girl like Taylor do on a Friday night when her boyfriend was out of town?

Carly was proud of herself when she decided against it.

And then the next thing she knew, she found herself walking across the street and pulling open the heavy glass door of the Monroe Gallery.

Found herself?

Yes. Found herself. As much as she had tried, in the days that had elapsed since, to locate the point in time where she made the fateful decision to enter the gallery, she couldn't. She knew full well that she had made a choice to do what she did, to go where she'd gone. She had only herself to blame. But she could not recall making the decision. One minute she was averting catastrophe, heading back to her life—such as it was. And the next she was creating catastrophe.

She felt a jolt of alarm when she saw the uniformed guard standing next to the reception desk. But he smiled and nodded at her, like she was just one of the crowd. And so Carly walked on, trying to look like she belonged there as much as anyone did.

A waitress in a white shirt and black bow tie offered cheese-stuffed mushrooms. Carly was too nervous to eat, but when a waiter came by seconds later with a tray of plastic champagne flutes, she took one and downed it. The bubbles tickled her nose, and as she swallowed, she felt the warmth travel down her throat, across her chest, and right up to her head.

She made her way to the back of the room, where a

huge painting illuminated from above and below had the whole wall to itself. On her way, she met the champagne-carrying waiter again and exchanged her empty plastic flute for a full one.

The painting was called *Lucinda*. At first she wondered about the name, since all she could see was an old house with cracked windows and peeling paint surrounded by trees. But then her eye landed on the upstairs window, where a shadowy figure peered out into the trees. Carly stepped closer and saw that the figure was a woman and she was naked—or at least the part you could see was naked. Whoever said "haunting and disturbing" on the artdealers.org Web site was right. *Lucinda* exuded sadness. There was a car in the driveway below, but the woman seemed very much alone, cut off from the rest of the world. But maybe she wasn't alone, Carly thought. Maybe there was a husband or a boyfriend lying asleep on a bed behind her. Maybe there was a baby dreaming in the room behind the next window.

According to the tiny card on the wall, *Lucinda* cost $50,000.

"I can't believe this. Her work is so facile. So derivative. Hello? Anyone ever hear of Edward Hopper?"

The source of this pronouncement was a skinny blue-haired woman in a black sack of a dress. She was standing a few feet away from Carly, arms crossed tightly, scowling at the painting. At first Carly thought the woman was talking to her, but then someone else said, "I know. Ever since MoMA put her in that nineties retrospective . . ."

The source of that comment was an even skinnier pasty-faced guy wearing a faded Mr. Bubble T-shirt. He said it loud enough for anyone in his immediate vicinity to hear.

They moved on to trash the next painting. Carly had no idea if the work was derivative or the artist was over-rated. She liked *Lucinda*. She didn't think she'd want to look at it all day every day. It was too sad. But if she had that kind of money, she figured, she'd probably have a big house, and she could keep *Lucinda* in her own quiet corner, a place reserved for sadness.

While Carly stood there, imagining a house with a room for her every mood, someone else came up beside her and said, "This is my favorite." She'd already turned her head toward the familiar voice before remembering she wasn't supposed to know or be known by anyone in that room. It was Judith Deen, Taylor's mother. And she was smiling at Carly. "It says so much about loneliness and longing, don't you think?"

"Yeah," she said. "It does." Was that a trap, a trick question? She scanned the room for the nearest exit.

"I'm tempted to buy it myself."

"Too late!" The little blonde receptionist seemed to come out of nowhere. She reached out and placed a sticker, a tiny red dot, on the price tag. She turned to Judith with a big smile.

"Who?" Judith asked.

"Jack Chiara," said the receptionist.

"Good for Jack," said Judith, looking around the gallery, which was quite crowded by now. "Where is he?" The two of them walked off in search of the $50,000 man.

Carly was safe. Judith had no idea who she was.

She continued down the hallway at the back of the gallery, which led to a glass door with JUDITH MONROE DEEN painted in long, gold letters. Carly glanced into the darkened room before turning around. A single red light— a phone, a computer, maybe an alarm—blinked on and off. She headed back up the hall, passing pairs and groups of people talking in low whispers.

At the end of the hall was another door made of dark solid wood. At its center was a gold plate engraved with the word PRIVATE.

As Carly passed, the door opened. A waiter carrying a tray of grilled shrimp on skewers came out.

He paused and held the tray out for her. "Shrimp?"

"No, thanks," she said.

He nodded and disappeared down the hall without bothering to close the door behind him.

Carly took a few steps back and peered into the stairway behind the door. Two more waiters were on their way down with trays.

"He claims they're not," said the first to come through the door. His tray held tiny crackers dotted with tiny blobs of some pinkish-orange thing. When he saw Carly, he held it out to her. "Salmon mousse?"

She shook her head and he moved on as the other came out saying, "But you *know* they are." He stopped in front of Carly and lowered his tray, "Champagne?"

Carly reached for her third small plastic fluteful of champagne, courtesy of the Monroe Gallery, est. 1963.

"Thanks."

He left the door ajar. Carly waited a moment in case there were more waiters. When none came, she pushed the door open and peered in on a narrow stairway leading into the family home.

The wall along the narrow stairway was covered with framed photographs. She glanced up and down the hallway. Seeing no one, stepped over the threshold. Her predictable heart started its predictable pounding. She tried to calm it by telling herself she hadn't done anything that bad. If anyone asked, all she had to do was say she was looking for the bathroom.

She drank the champagne in one long gulp and took three deep, calming breaths as she stepped toward the pictures. This wasn't Monroe Gallery art; it was Monroe family history. From the bottom to the top, the wall was covered in snapshots of Taylor's grandparents and their famous artist friends, Judith as a baby, a young girl, and a bride. Big next to small. Old next to new. Black-and-white next to vivid and faded color. One double frame held two pictures, mirror images of mothers and baby daughters under the same striped umbrellas on a white-sand beach. The "rustic island getaway" in Jamaica. The first, Sadie and Judith; the second, Judith and Taylor.

As she climbed those stairs leading from the open-to-the-public Monroe Gallery to the clearly demarcated private living space of the Deen family, Carly wasn't thinking about how the criminal code of the State of New York would view her actions. All she wanted was a glimpse into the perfect life of the perfect girl who had taken her place. Which isn't to say she didn't know what she was doing. Or had somehow lost the capacity to judge right from wrong. No. She knew what she was doing. She knew it was wrong. But once she had started up those stairs, she could not stop. Maybe if the State of New York criminal code had sent a messenger, a spokesperson in the form say, of Susan G. Whitman, Esq., to intervene, to read her the part about how what she was doing *could* cost her a $500 fine, three months in jail, and/or a year's probation, well maybe then she would have stopped.

It was easy to sit in the conference room of Babcock & Whitman, Attorneys-at-Law, and ask, as her mother was now, what the hell she thought she was doing going into *those people's home*. The best response Carly could think of was that she wasn't really thinking at all as she stepped farther and farther down the road that led to that order of protection and the possibility of criminal charges they were gathered around the table to discuss.

"Curious" doesn't quite capture the feeling that kept her moving up those stairs past the original of that picture the *Times* Home section had carried of the pregnant Judith and her husband resting their hands on her swollen belly.

She was almost to the top of the stairs when she heard someone behind her say, "Excuse me." She whipped her head around, ready to make excuses about looking for bathrooms, opening wrong doors. But it was just another waiter, this one with an empty tray, wanting to get by. He didn't give her a second look when she backed up against the banister to let him by. And when he took a left at the top of the stairs, toward the sound of clanging pans and the smells of elegant finger food, she turned right and found herself in a softly lit, painting-lined hallway that opened into a big, dark room. There was enough light coming in through the windows for her to see a big couch and some chairs next to a huge fireplace and to see that there was a man sitting in one of the chairs.

"Taylor?" His voice was deep. A bit ragged.

"No. Sorry. I must have taken a wrong turn. I was looking for the kitchen."

The bathroom excuse wasn't going to work up here. And so on the spur of the moment she made herself into a clueless member of the catering staff. It was lame. From the top of the stairs there was no question which direction the kitchen was. And the staff was obviously very professional. Not to mention that her cargo pants and T-shirt looked nothing like the black dress pants, white shirts, and black bow ties they wore.

But the man in the chair wasn't asking questions. He had needs of his own.

"Wait. Young lady?" She heard the clicking of a lamp.

She turned around to find a red-faced R. Conrad "Duffy" Deen III sitting in a blue blazer and a crumpled, open-collared, violet shirt. He was holding an empty wine bottle out to her. "Would you get me another bottle of this fine vintage?"

It was clear from the way he spoke—too slow, too loud—that R. Conrad "Duffy" Deen III had consumed that entire bottle on his own.

"I—uh—"

"I'd get it myself, but I'm supposed to stay out of the way." He looked around the room like he didn't quite know how he got there.

"Um, sure. Let me just—" She walked toward him, took the bottle out of his hand, and pretended to inspect the label. "I'll just—um—"

"Thank you, thank you very much," he said with a sigh as he reached for the lamp switch.

Carly followed the little bit of light down the hallway

to the bustling kitchen. A chef in checked pants and white linen jacket was arranging trays of hors d'oeuvres for waiting waiters.

"Um, excuse me," she said to the waiter closest to the door. She held the bottle out. "Could someone—Um, Mr. Deen asked for another bottle of wine? He's in the living room?" She tilted her head behind her.

The waiter laughed, took the empty bottle, and tossed it into a bin on the floor, the clank barely audible over the bustle of the kitchen.

"Duffy wants more," he yelled to a woman slicing lemons at the back of the room.

"Don't give it to him!"

The waiter turned back to Carly and shrugged. "Don't worry. He'll pass out and forget. He always does."

Whether Duffy was passed out or just resting, he didn't stop Carly when she tiptoed past the room down the hall where she thought the bedrooms should be. There was no question of stopping now. She'd made it all the way up the stairs. People had seen her and hadn't flipped out. No one had asked her who she was, what she was doing upstairs. She'd seen Taylor leave the building. It looked like she and her friends were on their way out for the night. That was less than an hour ago.

Now it was just a matter of figuring out which of the four doors led to Taylor's room.

It was the second door Carly tried. The room was huge, as Carly had expected. But messy, as she hadn't. She stepped inside and quietly shut the door behind her. It was only in size that Taylor Deen's inner sanctum met any of Carly's expectations. Whenever she'd imagined Taylor's room, she'd seen a magazine spread with designer furniture, luxury bedding, and expensive rugs. Never any clutter or dirty clothes. And certainly no plates with food scraps like the one piled with shrimp tails on the desk. In Carly's imagination, Taylor's bed was always made, the clothes were always put away.

Taylor's big bed did have an expensive-looking duvet and sheets, but they were all twisted into a huge clump in the center, and the bed itself was covered with clothes, books, and magazines.

The only place Carly could sit down was in the big, overstuffed easy chair in an alcove with double dormer windows. She made her way over to it and put her feet up on the ottoman. She sat with her hands over the worn patches on the arms. The fabric was velvety and soft. But old. Threadbare at the arms. She wondered who else had rested their arms here. Brian? Bob Dylan when he was allegedly "romantically linked" with Taylor's grandmother? Out the window she could see the arch of Washington Square Park and wondered what it would have been like growing up with that view. Not bad, she thought. There would be lots of great people-watching from that spot. All those windows, lit up against the New York night. If she lived here, she'd spend hours in that chair, imagining the lives behind those windows.

Across from the chair was a desk with two huge, flat-screen monitors and a fancy, ergonomically correct chair on wheels. Hanging from the back of the chair was Taylor's deep-red sweater, the one she wore the day Carly followed her. Carly left the easy chair for the Aeron, placing a hand on the sweater as she did so. It was even softer than it looked. Carly picked it up and turned it inside out, searching for the label, which verified that it was indeed one hundred percent cashmere. She held it to her cheek and breathed in Taylor's orange-mixed-with-cinnamon scent. With the sweater in her lap, she touched the mouse, and the screen came to life, bathing the room in purple-blue light.

Taylor's desktop was a collage of her photographs. Some were familiar to Carly, like the black-and-white "Gig" series where she'd seen her breakup with Brian caught for posterity. Others were new to her—scenes of destroyed houses in New Orleans, one of Taylor's mother standing on her head in yoga class, one of her father looking much better rested, less crumpled, and less drunk than he did out in the living room.

And then up in the corner, a weird sort of portrait of Brian inside a hand-drawn frame. It was a terrible picture. It was badly lit. His hair looked like it hadn't been combed or brushed. Carly wondered why, when she had so many great pictures of Brian, Taylor would want to look at this one every time she turned on her computer. It looked almost like a mug shot the way he was staring dully into the camera.

And then he moved.

At first Carly thought she'd imagined it.

Then he moved again. He scratched his cheek and rubbed his nose, and she thought Taylor had put a couple pictures on a loop to create the illusion of movement.

But then he spoke. "Hey. You there? I thought you were going to that party." He wasn't looking into the camera but right below it. He was looking at a monitor. It wasn't a picture. It was a live video stream.

His face came even closer to the monitor. "Taylor?" Until then, Carly had been so focused on the screen that she hadn't noticed the glowing green light at the top of Taylor's monitor. That meant—

"God, this is really weird. . . ." Brian squinted. "You look like—"

Carly lowered her head and let her hair hang in front of her face. Her big curly red hair that Brian loved so much.

"Carly? What the—?"

Carly pulled the sweater from her lap and threw it over her head.

"Carly, what are you doing there?"

With the sweater covering her face, she slipped out of

the chair, got on her hands and knees, and crawled across the room toward the door to the sound of Brian yelling "Taylor? Carly? Taylor? Carly?" with increasing panic. She stopped once to look back at the monitor and she saw a freaked-out Brian on his phone, and Avery and Liam taking turns peering into the monitor.

She almost made it out. If she hadn't collided with the waiter and tray full of hot-from-the-oven cheese puffs, she probably would have been able to get down the stairs, through the crowd, and out the door. Of course they would have caught up with her eventually. If not that night, then the next day, or the day after that. Brian would have told them who she was and where to find her. It wouldn't have changed the trouble she was in, but it would have been less humiliating.

As soon as Brian realized he wasn't imagining things, that he was indeed seeing his ex-girlfriend inside the bedroom of his new girlfriend, he set in motion the series of events that led to Carly's being escorted out of the Monroe Gallery by two New York City police officers. Assuming the worst of the girl he'd last spoken to on the night she'd called his mother's house eight times, Brian called Taylor, who called her mother, who grabbed the rent-a-cop she always hired for these events and headed upstairs. And there Carly was, blocked from the stairs by the waiter and the chef and the woman who wouldn't let R. Duffy Deen III have another bottle of wine, all on their hands and knees hastily trying to gather up all the dripping Gruyère-stuffed phyllo dough before it stained the carpet.

"And the sweater?" Susan asked. As she had told Carly, the prosecutor was focusing on the fact that Carly was holding Taylor's sweater in her hand when she was caught. Stealing an item of clothing or some other token from the target was apparently "textbook stalker behavior."

"I *wasn't* stealing it. I was just—"

Carly stopped herself. There was no point in trying to explain.

EPILOGUE

Six Months Later

CARLY IS packing.

The duffel is going with her to Turkey. Two of the three boxes sitting on her futon are headed to Greenville, where they will be stored in her father's guest room/study until it's time to move into her dorm at Denman. The third box will go to the new apartment. A paper shopping bag filled with wearable clothes that no longer fit or interest her is marked for Goodwill. The plastic garbage bag will go down the chute into the compactor in the basement of the crappy sublet.

Almost everything has been sorted. One by one she's decided the destiny of her belongings. The only place left to clear is the bottom cubby of the wobbly IKEA unit she put together in September. It's packed with papers, random shoes, and she's not sure what else.

She starts with the shoes. Once-white sneakers, now gray and scuffed. A pair of blue ballet flats she never wore except at school.

Garbage.

Next, a balled-up regulation navy-blue Bellwin V-neck.
She wants to put that in the garbage, too. But she won't.
She'll give it to her mother, who'll have it dry-cleaned and
pass it along discretely to one of the girls who wear Payless
shoes and shop at "the Marts." And here's her other winter
kilt. She'd wondered where that went. Isabelle will take care
of that, too. Make sure it gets to someone who needs it.

Under all that she finds a hat she almost doesn't rec-
ognize. Then she does. An ugly, brown knit wool hat with
something—the turquoise reading glasses—inside. Beneath the hat, a pile of old school papers and tests and
then a notebook. Her Harriet the Spy notebook, which,
unlike Harriet's, never fell into the wrong hands and so
didn't further complicate the complicated-enough mess
that was her life six months before.

What will she do with all this? The hat is easy enough.
She'd pilfered it from her mother's Goodwill bag in the
first place. So back it goes. The glasses? She throws those
in the Goodwill bag, too. She paid about ten dollars for
them at a drugstore. Maybe some old lady who actually
needs them to read will be happy to get them for a dollar
or two. Or maybe they'll become part of someone's Hal-
loween costume in the fall. Or maybe someone in search
of a cheap and easy disguise will find them.

And the notebook? What will she do with that bit of
evidence? Should she go to Riverside Park and burn it?
Would she get in trouble for that? Maybe mixed-paper

recycling, where her words, all that dangerous information about Taylor Deen and her seemingly perfect life will get churned to pulp and reincarnated as . . . what? Environmentally correct paper towels? A clever greeting card printed on one hundred percent post-consumer recycled paper? Pages that bear witness to some other teenage girl's worst missteps?

"Missteps" was Susan G. Whitman, Esq.'s word. She'd also used "poor choices," "bad decisions," "clouded thinking," and "mistakes" in her correspondence with the Deen family attorney and the prosecutor.

In the face of the incontrovertible evidence, Susan had said the only thing they could do was ask for compassion. She asked them to consider whether Carly's missteps were deserving of the criminal record that would be with her for the rest of her life if charges were pressed. Everyone agreed that prosecution would be taking it too far in this case, with a girl who had never been in trouble before. But Judith Monroe Deen still wanted that order of protection. When she learned that her daughter's boyfriend's ex-girlfriend had unlawfully entered her daughter's bedroom, Judith was seriously freaked out. She wanted legal action of some kind.

Carly didn't want to fight it. Part of her agreed with Judith. Who could blame a mother for wanting to protect her child from a possible lunatic? But Susan pointed out that even without formal charges, simply having her name on such a document could cause Carly serious future grief.

Through Susan, Isabelle and Tim and Nick convinced Judith that they, as her parents, would personally restrain Carly. They would see to it that she didn't come anywhere near the Monroe Gallery and Deen house. Fourteenth Street, where Nick lived, was as far downtown as Carly was allowed to go for the next six months. Judith agreed, with the stipulation that if Carly was spotted anywhere near Taylor, the authorities would be notified and the Deens would pursue "every legal avenue" to protect Taylor.

That was fine because by then Carly didn't need restraining. She was done. She didn't want to see Taylor or Brian or know anything about what they were doing, how things were going between them, any of it.

Humiliation will do that to a person.

Susan sent Carly to a psychologist for evaluation, to help make her case to the prosecutor. After hearing the story of how her obsession with Taylor started and grew, the shrink recommended that Carly take a good long break from the Web. Not as a punishment, but a precautionary measure, Dr. Stavros explained. All that information just a click away could "trigger" Carly's "compulsive tendencies." And given her inability to stop herself from acting, Dr. Stavros thought it would be best if the laptop was made completely unavailable to Carly.

She surrendered it to her mother and did manage—despite her initial protests—to get through her final semester working entirely with books, paper, pens and pencils, plus occasional, limited, and closely supervised forays onto the Internet for legitimate research purposes only.

The months immediately following her non-breaking and entering were hard. Word of her "poor choices" spread through Bellwin immediately. She had the experience of briefly being the *cause célèbre du jour*. Whispers, laughter, knowing looks. The whole bit. Word spread to other schools, too. Harris Gibson pretended he didn't know Carly when they passed on the street. Shira Zeidman wrote it up on her blog, in a post titled "The Further Adventures of Little Miss Psycho."

But eventually, Carly's infamy faded, overshadowed by Chloe Brosnan's arrest for buying heroin on the Lower East Side two months later.

Val stuck by her through all of it. After everything was settled with the lawyers, and Carly was finally allowed contact with the outside world, the first person she called—the only person she *wanted* to call—was Val. But she wasn't sure Val would answer. Carly wouldn't have blamed her if she'd wanted to keep her distance. So it was a huge relief when after only one ring she heard her friend's voice. Carly didn't care that there was no "hello." No "How are you?" Just an angry, very Val-like "What the hell?!"

The thing that bothered Val the most was how Carly had lied and kept secrets.

"I could have stopped you, you know. If you'd just told me."

"I know. That's why I didn't tell you. It sounds crazy now, but it all made sense at the time. I was messed up."

"Yes, you were."

Val was the one to tell Carly about "The Stalker Girl Song." It wasn't Ernestine is Everywhere's. It was put out by a Canadian band called Uncle Buddy. But, Val told her, it made mention of enough details—like the red sweater and Bernie Williams and somebody calling somebody's mom—to conclude that Brian was at least the source of the story, if not the ghostwriter of the song.

Carly guesses, but hasn't verified because it would mean going online, that Uncle Buddy and EiE crossed paths on tour. She hasn't heard the song yet. She's waiting for the day when it will all seem funny. Which might be never.

She's turning the notebook over in her hand, wondering if she's brave enough to peek inside, when her phone rings. The caller ID says DAD.

"Hey Dad."

"Whoa, is this my daughter live and in person?"

"Who were you expecting?"

"Oh, I don't know. Your voice mail. Hold on a sec," he says. She hears her baby sister Ally gurgling, followed by some muffled sounds, and then the crash of the phone hitting the floor. After a few seconds, he's back. "Still there?"

"Still here."

"Oh, okay. Sorry about that. I had to turn Ally around in the Baby Bjorn. When she's awake, she wants to face out and see the world." His voice goes into a higher pitch as he says, "Isn't that right, little girl? You want to know what's goin' on, don'tcha?"

Carly smiles as she listens to her father dote. "How's my little sister?"

"Great. You should see her, Carl. She's so curious. So *here*."

Professor Tim Finnegan is on paternity leave, and he's taking it very seriously. He's not teaching, not writing, not going to department meetings. Just his getting to know his new daughter.

He's read all the books, and he's convinced that Ally is a genius. She's hit every developmental milestone ahead of time. She rolled over at thirteen weeks, well ahead of the national norm. Ditto for the crucial skills of reaching and grasping. He swears he hears words in her babbles and squeaks. He still e-mails Carly pictures almost every day. The most recent was of the two of them "reading" a book. Actually, Ally was drooling onto the book and Tim had a maniacal, wide-eyed look on his face as he pointed to the pictures and read aloud.

"That's great. Tell her I say 'hey.'"

"Here, tell her yourself."

Carly laughs and shakes her head. "Dad, wait!" But it's too late. She can hear Ally breathing and babbling on the other end.

"Hi, Ally," she says. "I hope for your sake this is just a phase. I can't really say because I didn't live with him after the age of four."

Carly listens to two more squeaks and one grunt and then says, "Okay, well. Can you put Dad back on? Dad? Dad!"

"I'm here. She knows your voice. I really think she does. Her whole face lit up when you were talking."

"Really?"

"Really. She can't wait to see you. I just thought of a few more things."

"Dad. I'm totally ready. I was ready a year ago."

"I know. But I was thinking, are you sure your shots are still up-to-date? Because some of them might have expired."

"Yes, I'm sure. Mom double-checked today."

"And you got the hat?"

"Yes, Dad. The hat, the sunscreen, the tampons."

Jess pokes her head through the flimsy blue drapes. She has a flower painted on her cheek, a remnant from the Bellwin all-school end-of-the-year picnic that afternoon in Central Park.

"Can we go?"

Carly nods. "Dad—I have to go. I'll see you in a few days."

It's Friday, and she and Jess are due down at Nick's within the hour for their regular Friday-night pizza-movie-sleepover.

Not long after Carly's "bust," Nick and Isabelle decided that Carly should be included in the weekend visits with Jess. Carly didn't have any say in the matter, since she had pretty much agreed to give up her free will in exchange for Judith's dropping her demands for a restraining order. But that was okay. She liked this decision they made for her. After all that had happened, she was afraid Nick might not want anything to do with her. She'd heard from her mother that Nick and Judith had mutual acquaintances in the art world, and she worried that she might have hurt his career.

But Nick's career seems to be going just fine. Nick has a show out in Los Angeles coming up that summer.

Carly likes the ritual of their Friday nights: first taking the subway downtown with Jess, then the three of them picking out a video together and on the way back to the loft getting their pizza. She and Nick recently revived the DTM, "Don't Tell Mom," when they let Jess watch an R-rated movie. Nick had already seen it and knew that it didn't have any sex or violence.

"Just Irish people who drop a lot of f-bombs, which

you can hardly even hear because of their accents," he said in a bad Irish brogue.

Isabelle seems to be making better use of her weekend nights, too. She's started going to readings and other literary things around the city. She's not exactly cheery, but she seems to be coming out of her funk. Tonight she's staying home to finish packing.

She's found a better, if not perfect, apartment. One of Val's aunts is going back to Puerto Rico to open a branch of the family restaurant—NYSJ—and subletting her two-bedroom to Isabelle. It's still temporary, but they expect it to be at least two years. And it has the added advantage of being upstairs from Val. Maybe she and Carly will avoid the fate of so many high-school friends who drift apart when they leave for college.

"Yes, let's go," Carly says to Jess. She reaches over, opens the zipper on her Turkey-bound duffel, and slips the notebook in. She's not ready to read this artifact from her not-so-distant past. She's not sure she ever will be. But she's not going to destroy it, either.

There's a lot to be learned from the past. And there are still a lot of blank pages.

ACKNOWLEDGMENTS

Huge thanks to Tracey Adams of Adams Literary for her patience and wise counsel, and to Joy Peskin for saying "No," then "No," and then "Yes!" Thanks to Nancy Brennan for designing a cover that captures the story so well; to Janet Pascal (and Janet Frick) for making me think about every word; and to the sales and marketing folks at Penguin Young Readers Group for their energy and enthusiasm.

A fellowship at Hedgebrook on Whidbey Island in Washington State provided quiet space as well as the jovial company of other women writers. I found quiet inspiration in the Placitas, New Mexico, home of Deb Green and Jerry Blakely when my friend Deborah Davis let me tag along on her annual writing retreat—twice. The women of Word of Mouth–Bay Area provided good food, challenging conversation, and above all, the inspiration to keep at it no matter what.

— — —

Several people provided generous reads and helpful notes despite the mess they were handed. Thank you Lou Berney, Elizabeth Stark, Ellen Sussman, and Laura Ruby. Elaine Korry convinced me to give it one more try when I'd all but given up. My sister, Ellen Gehrs, might not know how much her encouragement means to me. Members of Tyler Gehrs' high school band may hear echoes of their songs in EiE's.

Finally, my husband, Kevin Griffin, and our daughter, Graham Griffin, loved and supported me even at my crankiest. They did without me for days—sometimes weeks—and celebrated when we finally got to "Yes!"